TORMENT

THE CLASSIC HANK JANSON

The first original Hank Janson book appeared in 1946, and the last in 1971. However, the classic era on which we are focusing in the Telos reissue series lasted from 1946 to 1953. The following is a checklist of those books, which were subdivided into five main series and a number of 'specials'.

PRE-SERIES BOOKS
When Dames Get Tough (1946)
Scarred Faces (1947)

SERIES ONE
1) This Woman Is Death (1948)
2) Lady, Mind That Corpse (1948)
3) Gun Moll For Hire (1948)
4) No Regrets For Clara (194)
5) Smart Girls Don't Talk (1949)
6) Lilies For My Lovely (1949)
7) Blonde On The Spot (1949)
8) Honey, Take My Gun (1949)
9) Sweetheart, Here's Your Grave (1949)
10) Gunsmoke In Her Eyes (1949)
11) Angel, Shoot To Kill (1949)
12) Slay-Ride For Cutie (1949)

SERIES TWO
13) Sister, Don't Hate Me (1949)
14) Some Look Better Dead (1950)
15) Sweetie, Hold Me Tight (1950)
16) Torment For Trixie (1950)
17) Don't Dare Me, Sugar (1950)
18) The Lady Has A Scar (1950)
19) The Jane With The Green Eyes (1950)
20) Lola Brought Her Wreath (1950)
21) Lady, Toll The Bell (1950)
22) The Bride Wore Weeds (1950)
23) Don't Mourn Me Toots (1951)
24) This Dame Dies Soon (1951)

SERIES THREE
25) Baby, Don't Dare Squeal (1951)
26) Death Wore A Petticoat (1951)
27) Hotsy, You'll Be Chilled (1951)

28) It's Always Eve That Weeps (1951)
29) Frails Can Be So Tough (1951)
30) Milady Took The Rap (1951)
31) Women Hate Till Death (1951)
32) Broads Don't Scare Easy (1951)
33) Skirts Bring Me Sorrow (1951)
34) Sadie Don't Cry Now (1952)
35) The Filly Wore A Rod (1952)
36) Kill Her If You Can (1952)

SERIES FOUR
37) Murder (1952)
38) Conflict (1952)
39) Tension (1952)
40) Whiplash (1952)
41) Accused (1952)
42) Killer (1952)
43) Suspense (1952)
44) Pursuit (1953)
45) Vengeance (1953)
46) Torment (1953)
47) Amok (1953)
48) Corruption (1953)

SERIES 5
49) Silken Menace (1953)
50) Nyloned Avenger (1953)

SPECIALS
Auctioned (1952)
Persian Pride (1952)
Desert Fury (1953)
One Man In His Time (1953)
Unseen Assassin (1953)
Deadly Mission (1953)

TORMENT

HANK JANSON

This edition first published in the United Kingdom in 2003 by
Telos Publishing Ltd, 17 Pendre Avenue, Prestatyn, LL19 9SH
www.telos.co.uk

Telos Publishing Ltd values feedback. Please e-mail us with
any comments you may have about this book to:
feedback@telos.co.uk

This edition © 2013 Telos Publishing Ltd
Introduction © 2003 Steve Holland
Novel by Stephen D Frances
Cover by Reginald Heade
With thanks to Steve Holland - www.hankjanson.co.uk
Silhouette device by Philip Mendoza

ISBN: 978-1-84583-866-9

The Hank Janson name, logo and silhouette device are
trademarks of Telos Publishing Ltd

First published in England by New Fiction Press, April 1953

British Library Cataloguing in Publication Data.
A catalogue record for this book is available from the British
Library.

Telos edition dedicated to Jennifer Janson, with regards from her 'Uncle Hank'

PUBLISHER'S NOTE

The appeal of the Hank Janson books to a modern readership lies not only in the quality of the storytelling, which is as powerfully compelling today as it was when they were first published, but also in the fascinating insight they afford into the attitudes, customs, modes of expression and, significantly, morals of the 1940s and 1950s.

We have therefore endeavored to make *Torment*, and all our other Hank Janson reissues, as faithful to the original edition as possible. Unlike some other publishers who, when reissuing vintage fiction, have been known to make editorial changes to remove aspects that might offend present-day sensibilities, we have left the original narrative absolutely intact. So if, in the original edition, Hank made, say, a casually sexist remark about women – as he does on occasion in *Torment* – then that is what you will read in the Telos edition as well.

That's just the kinda guy Hank was.

Which brings us to a point about language. The original editions of these classic Hank Janson titles made quite frequent use of phonetic 'Americanisms' such as 'kinda', 'gotta', 'wanna' and so on. Again, we have left these unchanged in the Telos reissues, to give readers as genuine as possible a taste of what it was like to read these books when they first came out, even though such devices have since become sorta out of fashion.

The only way in which we have amended the original text has been to correct obvious lapses in spelling, grammar and punctuation – we have, for instance, added question marks in the not-infrequent cases where they were omitted from the ends of questions in the original – and to remedy clear typesetting errors.

Lastly, we should mention that we have made every effort to trace and acquire relevant copyrights in the various elements that make up this book. If anyone has any further information that they could provide in this regard, however, we would be very grateful to receive it.

INTRODUCTION

Torment was the forty-sixth novel to appear under the Hank Janson byline, originally published in the spring of 1953. Since his novel debut in 1948 (leaving aside the two novellas in 1946), Janson had sold five million copies of his books, making him Britain's fastest selling crime writer[1].

To split hairs, 'writer' is technically wrong — it's a minor semantic distinction of which Janson's creator, Stephen Frances, was aware, and by which he was amused. Frances was a two-finger typist whose skills in that direction never improved in forty years. His correspondence was littered with corrections, scribbled inserts and postscripts, made worse after Frances purchased a faulty electric typewriter that the manufacturers could not fix and would not allow him to return. His letters were a perfect example of how he allowed words simply to pour out, getting his thoughts down on paper as quickly as he could and only later

---

[1] Although James Hadley Chase, author of the notorious *No Orchids For Miss Blandish*, had higher cumulative sales, his 32 novels (at that time) had appeared over fourteen years to Janson's five.

The original edition of *Torment* was the first book to feature this slightly embellished version of the distinctive 'silhouette' logo, which was then adopted for subsequent titles.

going back to worry about making them grammatically correct.

When Frances began producing the Hank Janson novels in 1948 he was faced with a problem: he had limited capital with which to establish himself as a publisher after the collapse of his former venture, Pendulum Publications. A deal with Gaywood Distributors meant that once the books were published, he could sell the whole print run, but he was still involved in the time-consuming business of arranging covers, finding paper, getting his books printed, paying bills and a thousand and one other chores. It was taking him three weeks to poke out a novel on a typewriter.

The solution was called an Emidicta, a dictation / transcription machine that recorded onto wax cylinders, later replaced with an updated model that recorded onto magnetic paper discs. Locked away in his flat in London, Frances could dictate a novel in a week, taking the fifty or so discs he'd produced to a secretarial agency to have them transcribed. As each chapter appeared, he would make minor corrections, and a printer-ready manuscript could be produced in half the time it took for him to type.

Frances had discovered the quiet seaside village of Rosas during a holiday in Spain and decided to move there in 1951. Even during visits to see how the building work on his flat was progressing, Frances needed to keep dictating. With the blinds closed against the hot morning sun, he lay back in his room at the Mar y Sol hotel and told, quickly and passionately, his latest story of lust and murder, rewinding the Emidicta occasionally to check the recording.

On one occasion, the dialogue heard through the walls by a neighbour sounded suspicious and Frances was interrupted by two Civil Guards who kicked open the hotel door and levelled their sub-machine guns at him, expecting to find a foreign spy and a two-way radio …

In the heat of dictation, Frances *was* Hank Janson. And, conversely, Hank Janson was Frances poured out on the page, Janson's character sharing Frances's passions and obsessions. No wonder he felt hurt when, in 1954, he heard his alter ego declared to be obscene in an open court.

At the time when Frances was writing *Torment* in

The cover painting for *Torment* reflected a familiar theme in artist Reginald Heade's work: that of a bound or prone woman of remarkable beauty menaced by an unseen or shadowy male figure. Pictured here is another example of a 'gangster digest' falling within this sub-genre. Some of these titles are so rare that the number of copies in existence are believed to be in single figures.

AID THE FLOOD VICTIMS !

Read . . .

**Britain's
Great Flood Disaster**
(in pictures)

By HANK JANSON   PRICE 2/6

PROFITS DONATED
TO THE FUND FOR
FLOOD VICTIMS

Hank Janson your favourite author, writes an account of the Great Floods that rendered 30,000 homeless.

Buy this book and help the flood victims as well as providing yourself with a valuable record in words and pictures of an historic event.

Send 2/6 Postal Order to
New Fiction Press Limited
13½ Borough High Street, London, S.E.1.

Name..

Address...

This advert appeared in the back of the original edition of *Torment*, publicizing what must surely be the most unusual title to appear under the Hank Janson name. *Britain's Great Flood Disaster* was a largely photographic book, published in the same month as *Torment*, designed to raise money for victims of a catastrophic flood – reckoned to be Britian's worst for 600 years – that hit the East Coast of England on 1st February 1953.

1953, he had recently been in court. Facing the Borough Magistrates at Darwen, Frances had tried to defend his novel *The Jane With Green Eyes*, agreeing that the book was outspoken, but arguing that that did not necessarily make it obscene. The argument held little sway, and he was found guilty on two count of writing obscene books[2].

The Janson novels were aimed not at a sophisticated audience but at the widest audience possible. The books were not sexually explicit and Frances addressed that fact using Janson as a mouthpiece on more than one occasion, notably in *Torment for Trixie* and here in *Torment*. In *Torment for Trixie*, Janson addresses a meeting that has been called following the publication of a 'dirty' book, telling the audience that the words on the printed page are not in

---

[2] The second novel, *Milady Took The Rap*, Frances chose not to defend as it had already been prosecuted in Darwen and Editions Poetry (London) Ltd, the publisher, fined £100.

Britain's Great Flood Disaster is also probably the rarest Hank Janson title of all. Until the recent acquisition of this copy by Telos Publishing Ltd, it was generally believed that none survived.

themselves obscene, just made obscene by the interpretation put on them by dirty-minded readers; in *Torment*, Betty Scott has a notion, based on reading his novels, that Janson expects sex as a reward for his help, and Hank is forced to admit: 'Either you don't read good or I don't write good.'

Whether he admitted it in court or not, Frances knew his writing was sexually charged — he'd interrupt his dictation with asides to his secretary, 'Have you got hot pants yet, sweetie?' — and Hank becomes involved easily and often with women. Frances made his alter ego a 'sucker for dames,' especially cute-looking dames. The ideal Janson 'cute dame' has a beauty of the kind found in Greek sculpture; she is small, slim, well dressed, with an emphasis on low-cut tops that reveal the smooth white tops of breasts. Cleavage is a mysterious dark passage leading to untold promise and pleasure.

Women are often Janson's downfall. They tie him in knots, as you'll discover in his relationship with Betty Scott in *Torment*. Janson is trapped between desire and a personal moral code that makes him protect the underdog and never take advantage of the vulnerable; throughout the Janson saga, Hank rejects sex more often than he accepts it. Sometimes, his frustration leads to aggressive outbursts that might be considered sexual blackmail; at other times, Frances makes light of Hank's frustrations and relationships. Hank growls bitterly that he is having the usual kind of trouble — 'Women trouble.' A friendly doorman nods his head understandingly: 'I'm a married man myself.'[3]

Elsewhere in the narrative, Hank is disgusted at the sight of photographs: 'For two people alone in the world on their own that could have been something really special. But an intensely personal thing publicised in that blatant ugly fashion turned my guts over.' Read *Torment* and make up your own mind whether you think it plays to the sexual immaturity of Janson's supposed audience, or is a deliberately written cocktail of conflicting emotions that lifts the character of Hank Janson out of the ordinary.

Frances himself was raised in a matriarchal family, his early life dominated by his mother and maternal grandmother. The Janson books feature a steady parade of strong women and, in a series where obsession is often the dominant emotion, even the 'cute dames' that become victims have power.

The line between Hank Janson and Stephen Frances was constantly blurred, Janson reflecting his author's concerns far more openly than would normally be expected in what was, after all, cheap, pulp entertainment; Janson was still classed as 'gangster' fiction, a strange British sub-genre of the crime thriller, which grew up at a time when American imports were all but impossible to get hold of. Where American

---

[3] Frances was himself then recently divorced, although friendly cab drivers had been asking Janson about 'wife trouble' as far back as *Some Look Better Dead* in 1950.

audiences were reading Jim Thomson and Gil Brewer and others of that hardboiled ilk, British gangsters had developed out of a mixture of pre-WW2 American pulps, Carroll John Daly, W R Burnett and James M Cain, via British exponents of American hardboiled yarns, James Hadley Chase and Peter Cheyney. Most British gangster fiction has been forgotten, but Stephen Frances and Hank Janson have rightly endured in the memories of his readers, and novels like *Torment* show why.

Steve Holland
Colchester, February 2003

1

A city like Chicago is a big place where you can lose yourself with ease. Yet it's a small place too, because a guy who gets around as much as a reporter always finds himself bumping up against guys he knows or used to know.

So bumping into Billy Newman wasn't exactly a surprise.

He was standing at the bar when I first walked in. But it wasn't his broad shoulders that attracted my attention. It was the dame beside him; a cute little number with wide blue eyes and fair hair. I moved up to the counter right alongside her, ordered clearly so the dame would hear my voice. 'Make it a rye.'

That was when Billy saw me.

He kinda brushed the cute little number to one side, took me by the shoulder, turned me around and pumped my hand up and down. 'Hank! Well! Whad'ya know? Haven't set eyes on you in years. Say, fella, this is a *real* pleasure.'

'Holy smoke, Billy,' I said. 'Where you been keeping yourself?' I hadn't seen him in three years. The last time had been in a small West Coast town.

'You're looking swell, real swell,' he said with satisfaction, running his eyes over me.

'You're looking pretty good yourself,' I told him. He was too! Smartly dressed and looking kinda well-fed. The last time I'd seen him, he'd been shabby, hungry-looking and worried about his future. His future being the problem of next week's eating.

'Whad'ya doing now, Hank? Still writing?'

'I do a little reporting,' I told him modestly. 'I'm managing to hold down a job.'

His chest swelled just a little. 'I'm doing fine,' he said with satisfaction. '*Real* fine.'

My eyes flicked to the cute little number between us. He caught on immediately. 'Sorry,' he apologised. 'Should have introduced you before. This is Lucy. Lucy, meet Hank. A real fine guy.'

'Hiya, Lucy,' I said, and took her hand; cool slim fingers without a wedding ring. I looked into her eyes and they were a transparent blue like the Mediterranean. So transparent I could look deeper and deeper into them, crystal clear transparency that made me breathless, engulfed me, tempted me to allow myself to sink deeper and deeper. I'm a sucker for dames – cute looking dames. I let myself sink.

'Okay, okay, break it up,' chuckled Billy warningly. 'You wanna watch out for this guy, Lucy. He's a wolf.'

Slowly she withdrew her fingers from mine, switched her eyes from me to Billy. The numbness seeped out of me and I could breathe again. I grinned sheepishly. 'What's the matter, Billy? Scared of a little competition?'

A secretive smile tugged at her lips and she smiled at Billy, inviting him to answer me. He grinned broadly. 'You're way out of date, Hank. I'm married now. Married to the sweetest little girl you've ever met. Lucy's just my business associate.'

I looked at Lucy. Then I looked back at him. If Lucy was merely his business associate, his wife must surely be some dame.

He musta guessed the idea half-forming at the back of my mind. He said seriously: 'It's on the up and up, Hank. We really are business partners. I've been a proud father for eighteen months. That's the only reason my wife isn't on tour with us.'

'Still in show business then?' I asked. The last time I'd seen Billy, he'd been touring the third-rate variety theatres with a fourth-rate conjuring act, getting few bookings at that.

His eyes widened. 'Haven't you heard? We're playing the Casino.'

I thought he was ribbing me. The Chicago Casino is by no means a third-rate variety theatre. It's expensive and has a reputation for quality. Then once again I noticed his tailor-made clothes, his prosperous appearance and his air of satisfaction. 'You've made good then?' I said.

There was almost a fatherly air about the way he put his arm around Lucy's shoulders. '*We've* made good,' he said, and there was pride in his voice.

'It's a double act?'

'Yeah,' he said. 'We work under the name Los Guitanos. Making quite a name for ourselves, too.'

Part of my work involved knowing everything, skimming through newspapers from all parts of the States. The name Los Guitanos seemed vaguely familiar. 'I've heard of you,' I hazarded. 'Something about memory.'

His face was scandalised. 'You *don't know* our act? You've *never* seen us working together?'

I grinned wryly. It seemed he knew as little about my work as I did about his. 'Newspaper work makes you kinda busy,' I half-apologised.

He glanced at his watch, calculated swiftly. 'Doing anything special for the next coupla hours?'

I was. I had a cocktail party to attend to celebrate a well-known author's new publication. But Lucy looked at me, and there was something about those blue eyes ...

'What you got in mind?' I asked.

'We're on in twenty minutes,' he said. 'First show. Why not nip round and see the act?'

I thought quickly. The Casino was just around the corner. I could see the act, maybe date up Lucy and still get along to that cocktail party before it broke up.

'You've got me interested,' I said.

'Let's go then,' he said enthusiastically. 'Drink up and let's go.'

Naturally I was given one of the best seats and naturally I didn't have to pay.

I looked at the programme and saw Los Guitanos were given good billing, were the last act before the interval.

The curtain went down on a trick cycling act and I settled back in my seat more comfortably, waited with interest to see the curtain rise on Billy's act. But I wasn't kidding myself. It wasn't Billy I was interested in so much as Lucy.

Billy musta made good, I reasoned. The theatre

world is a tough world in which to make yourself a living. From my experience I'd learned that almost everyone is hypnotised by the bright lights, the desire to be publicly acclaimed and the centre of attraction. There are thousands of folks who try to hit the stage with an act that is mediocre. Therefore to pull oneself up above the general level requires real ability and determination.

When the curtain went up, I was tensed in my seat, anxious that Billy should put on a really good act.

The lighting was good and the slow lifting curtain revealed Billy in the centre of the darkened stage, spotlighted and seeming somehow mysterious and awe-inspiring. He wore evening dress and a silk hat. But the way he stood with his opera cloak draped around him and his arms folded across his chest, was dramatic and effective. There accompanied the music; a soft roll on the drums, which gave a background that was mysterious and dramatic.

The audience was hushed, tensed and silent and listening. Slowly, gracefully and with the audience now completely in his power, Billy spread his arms so that the black cloak draped him like a demon king who had sprung directly from the bowels of the Earth. He glided forward, swept his silk hat from his head, placed it crown downwards on the forefront of the stage and then retreated from it with dramatic, silently impressive movements.

Off stage Billy was a guy I knew, a regular guy who could tilt his elbow with the best of us. On the stage he was a dynamic, impressive figure, his eyes gleaming like those of a supernatural being, glowing with inspired power.

Slowly and dramatically he raised one white

hand, his black cloak billowing behind him. Then, abruptly, like casting a spell, his hand darted forward, seemed to throw in the direction of his silk hat. Amazingly the upturned hat spurted a tongue of red and yellow flame, a column of flame that leapt from the footlights, upwards and out of sight behind the safety curtain. Then, as the flame died, every light on the stage blazed into life, starkly outlining every nook and cranny, revealing Billy resplendent and handsome in his evening dress.

A ripple of applause greeted what was after all a well-staged but simple conjuring trick.

Billy bowed in acknowledgement of the scattered applause, advanced towards the footlights, paused until attentive silence was awaiting him, and then said in his rich, baritone voice:

'Ladies and gentlemen. Tonight it is my honour and my privilege to introduce Carmenita, the mystic girl possessed of supernatural powers who can see into the future, know the present and read the minds of a multitude.'

It was a nice build-up. When the drums began to roll and Lucy proudly and aloofly swept on to the stage, the audience's reaction had been well prepared.

She entered enveloped from head to toe in a black, flowing velvet robe. Like a queen, she advanced solemnly and seriously to the footlights, bowed and took the applause.

I applauded too. Not on account of Billy. On account of Lucy.

With the regal air of a queen, she took her position in the centre of the stage, and Billy spoke into the microphone, careful not to obstruct the audience's view of the queenly, regal Lucy as he said:

'Carmenita's powers are mysterious and beyond

dispute. No artificial aids are used to assist her in these demonstrations of her supernatural powers. It has been suggested that microscopic radio sets are used or other artificial methods are adopted in her demonstrations. Therefore, to ensure that her audience shall be convinced of the supernatural powers of Carmenita, we invite members of the audience to come up on stage as observers throughout the entire performance.'

There was a buzz among the audience. Lucy stood there, queenly and regal, staring in front of her like a being from another world. Somewhere over on my left, a young man got up from his seat, made towards the stage. Two or three others immediately followed suit, and an attendant guided them towards the stairway. There were two guys sitting next to me. One said: 'How about it?'

The other replied: 'Are you game?'

'Sure.'

'Come on then.'

In all, ten men and two women made their way to the stage before Billy indicated there were sufficient.

Seeing Billy on the stage was like seeing somebody I didn't know and had never met. Every movement he made was graceful and attention-inviting. He placed the observers on either side of Lucy, five men and one woman on each side, neatly spaced out so that Lucy remained the centre of interest. Lucy hadn't moved or blinked. She stared straight ahead of her into nowhere like a drugged woman.

'And now,' said Billy dramatically, *'we will ask our observers to assure themselves no artificial aids are being used.'*

With graceful movements, Billy went around back of Lucy, encircled her neck with his hands, pulled loose the bow of the cord that secured the black cloak, whisked it from her shoulders with a swift and graceful movement.

If the act had comprised nothing more than the revelation of Lucy, it would still have been a good act.

There was a kinda shocked sigh of approval from the audience as Lucy was starkly revealed beneath the probingly cruel spotlights. Yet she stood there queenly and serene with a dignity that made her revelation breath-taking and mind-shocking.

She was beautiful. She was a goddess! As Billy kinda slipped into the background and handed her cloak to a uniformed attendant who had come on the stage to receive it, the audience's eyes were centred on Lucy. She was a pocket-Venus, perfectly and beautifully sculptured, here skin warm with life and her body vital with femininity.

A slender strand of black silk stretched across her breasts, concealed only their pointedness, and a black silken thread around her loins held in position the fragile, black, silken G-string.

The audience gasped, stared at her breathtaking loveliness with an awed silence that reflected more than anything else the intensity of their interest.

Billy was experienced in stage craft. He waited a few seconds while the audience gaped; then in his rich, baritone voice he said softly: '*I will now ask the observers to scrutinise Carmenita, assure themselves there is no possibility whatsoever that there are hidden about her person or in her clothing, any artificial aid, microscopic radio sets or receivers.*'

Lucy was wearing maybe five square inches of

black silk. Tightly stretched silk at that, and barely concealing. But the ten guys up on the stage were smart enough not to let slip an opportunity like that. They circled around her, scrutinised her closely the way I would have done had I been up there with them, and finally, regretfully, reluctantly, they took up their positions on either side of her and assured the watching audience they could see no signs of any electrical appliances concealed about her person.

Meanwhile, Lucy stood there proud and aloof, staring in front of her, bathed in a kinda mystic detachment, oblivious to greedy, body-searching eyes, apparently quite remote and living in a mystical world of her own.

The observers remained on the stage while Billy, in his evening dress and flowing cloak, came down among the audience, took up his position in the centre gangway.

He said loudly, in a rich baritone voice that echoed around the theatre: '*Will one of the observers now kindly blindfold Carmenita.*'

A uniformed attendant came on to the stage, handed a black silk sash to one of the guys who had sat next to me. He was a young guy, all eyes. He advanced on Carmenita with a pleased grin spreading across his face. He unfolded the scarf, placed it carefully over Carmenita's eyes, wound it several times around her head before securing it.

'Now, sir,' asked Billy loudly from the gangway. 'You have examined that scarf. Will you assert it is quite opaque and that Carmenita is now unable to see anything happening around her?'

The fella's eyes kept flicking back to Lucy like they were magnetised. He nodded his head. 'She can't see a thing,' he confirmed. His voice seemed to say: '*But I can see plenty.*'

Billy asked the nearest person in the gangway: 'Will you kindly give me a personal article?'

It was a dame. She gave him a programme. Billy held it up. 'What is this?'

'A programme,' said Carmenita promptly in a low, emotionless voice.

'And this?' asked Billy. He was holding up a small, red book.

'A driving licence.'

'What is the number?'

'263214,' Lucy retorted immediately.

Billy returned the driving licence, took another card. 'And what is this?'

'A social security card.'

'Tell me, sir,' asked Billy, 'do you know the number?'

The man shuffled his feet uncomfortably. 'Afraid I can't.'

'Can you tell me the number, Carmenita?' asked Billy.

Speaking like she was in a dream, but without hesitation, she replied: '32751B-A.'

'Is that correct, sir?' asked Billy.

The man took back his security card, glanced at it, nodded his head with astonishment showing on his face.

'That's correct.'

In the space of the next few minutes, Carmenita described numbers and objects held up by Billy like she was reading them off. It was an amazing demonstration and I was beginning to understand Billy's rapid rise to success. I also had to acknowledge it that Billy's real success was due to Lucy. Physically she was astoundingly beautiful. Mentally she seemed possessed of powers that were supernatural.

Billy climbed back on to the stage. While he was speaking to the audience, an attendant wheeled in behind him a slender chromium and tubular framework, which was erected around Carmenita.

Billy said into the microphone: 'Last week in New Orleans, Carmenita looked into the future, prophesied the disaster that later overtook the fishing fleet that for a whole week was unable to leave the harbour.

'As one more demonstration of Carmenita's mystic powers, she will now be securely chained, yet without the knowledge of the audience will escape her shackles to prove once again her miraculous powers of telepathy.'

He turned back to Carmenita, took from the uniformed attendant two lengths of fine chain, which swiftly and skilfully he clamped around Carmenita's slender wrists. The other ends of the chains he placed in the hands of the four observers who were watching intently either side of Carmenita.

Carmenita, or Lucy as I knew her, stood calmly and serenely in the centre of the tubular framework, her arms extended either side of her, her wrists firmly tethered and the ends of the chains firmly held by the observers.

Billy asked two more members of the audience to come on to the stage.

His act was dramatic and effective. The two new members of the audience were asked to inspect a plain piece of white cardboard and initial it with their own initials. This blank white card was then placed by *them* in a black silk bag, the draw cord pulled so the bag was closed and the bag then hung around Carmenita's neck.

Billy said in his powerful, melodious stage voice: 'Now will the observers very gently take the strain upon the chains around Carmenita's wrists.'

They did so, straining her arms outwards so that her young, ripe body seemed to throb with life.

'And now ... the drapes!' announced Billy.

Once again the uniformed attendant, with whose help Billy draped Carmenita and the tubular frame. They covered her shoulders and the frame with a black silk drape that concealed her hands, arms and body down to her hips. Only the draw cord of the black bag around her neck was left in view.

Once again Billy came down into the audience. From the centre gangway he asked in a loud, ringing voice:

'Is anyone here in possession of a document bearing a number?'

There were fourteen offers.

Billy invited another member of the audience to select from the fourteen offers.

The selection was a birth certificate.

'Do you know the number of this?' asked Billy.

The owner of the birth certificate grinned ruefully. 'Afraid I don't.'

'You are required to give the number of this certificate,' said Billy.

Lucy nodded unseeingly but understandingly.

Billy wended his way back to the stage. With the aid of the attendant, he stripped away the black drapes, revealing that Lucy's arms were still extended either side of her, still tethered by the chains.

'This is very important,' Billy said to the observers in a loud, ringing voice. 'Are *all* of you quite sure you have kept a very careful hold on the chains?'

The observers grinned and nodded assurance. They appeared just a little awed.

'Very well,' said Billy. With a graceful, dignified gesture he invited two observers to remove the black bag from around Carmenita's neck.

They removed the bag, opened it up, drew out the piece of white cardboard they had initialled.

'Is there a number written on that cardboard?' asked Billy.

The observers looked at it, nodded wonderingly.

'Will you kindly read out the number?'

One of the observers stepped to the microphone, said into it: 'Number 635241.' His voice showed he knew this couldn't really be happening.

Billy confidently glanced down into the audience. 'Is that your number, sir?' he asked. 'Is that the number on your birth certificate?'

The guy with the birth certificate looked at it to confirm. 'That's dead right,' he agreed with a note of amazement in his voice. 'That's *dead* right!'

The applause was tremendous as Billy took a bow. Then the observers released their grip on the chains and Lucy shook her wrists free of restraint, took a bow herself.

I was applauding madly like all the others. But at the same time I was climbing up out of my seat.

Billy had invited me to visit them around back in his dressing-room after the show.

I was around back at his dressing-room so quick I arrived almost as soon as they did.

'Come in and make yourself at home,' invited

Billy genially. He opened a dressing-table drawer, pulled out a bottle of rye and papier-mâché cups.

It was a small dressing-room, two dressing-table mirrors with chairs placed in front of them, a settee and a screen.

Lucy's blue eyes smiled me a welcome, made me breathless. She was wearing that black velvet cloak, but she didn't disappoint me for long. As Billy poured, she seated herself before the mirror, untied the cloak, allowed it to fall back off her shoulders.

One the stage and way up above my head she had looked incredibly beautiful without the concealing cloak. Right close up where I could reach out and touch her, she was breathtakingly, tantalisingly desirable. And close up I could judge better because I could see more. That black silken strand across her breasts was barely wide enough to conceal the haloes. It held without restraining the youthful, vital exuberance of rounded, firm and prominent femininity.

The other silken strand strained around her loins low down, revealed the beautiful symmetry of hips, thighs and belly, made soft skin appear flushed, warm and throbbing with life. I watched with magnetised fascination as her youthful body moved smoothly and vitally as she spread cream on her face, cleaned away greasepaint.

'One for you, and one for you, my dear,' said Billy cheerfully as he deposited one cup in my hand, placed another at Lucy's elbow.

'What did you think of the show?' he asked confidently, knowing my answer in advance but wanting to bask in praise.

'Wonderful,' I told him, with sincerity. 'A first

class act. A pity it hasn't had the publicity it deserves. It's ... sensational!'

He frowned agreement. 'Yeah,' he said unhappily. 'We haven't had enough publicity. That's the trouble.'

My eyes were fixed on Lucy. Underarm I could see the rich swell of her firm breasts moving as she rubbed cream on her face. Just to be near her and watch her like that was giving me butterflies in the belly.

I said hoarsely, still without taking my eyes off Lucy: 'You musta worked hard to perfect that act. Maybe sometime you'll show me how you do it.'

He said seriously, a slightly shocked tone in his voice: 'It isn't a phoney act, Hank. It's genuine telepathy.'

I looked around at him, grinned and close one eye significantly.

His eyes were hurt. 'You've seen the act. There's no trickery about it.'

'Telepathy my foot,' I jeered.

He frowned. 'What do you think of hypnotism?' he demanded abruptly. 'David Stewart taught you how to do it, didn't he?'*

'That's different,' I defended. 'Hypnotism is a science. It's a physical accomplishment. But no scientist will yet agree that telepathy ...'

'I remember what you used to say about hypnotism, Hank,' he said seriously. 'You were sceptical. Damned sceptical. You claimed hypnotism

---

* In the original edition of *Torment*, there was at this point a footnote advertising one of the publisher's other titles: '*HYPNOTISM AND HOW TO DO IT' by DAVID STEWART* Price 8/6

was a stunt with stooges planted. But when David Stewart taught you how to do it, you just had to believe it then.'

He was right. I'd had to be taught how to hypnotise before I was willing to believe it could be done.

'And now you're being sceptical of telepathy,' he accused.

I stared at him solemnly. 'You're telling me your act is on the level?'

He nodded towards Lucy. 'She's the power,' he said dramatically. 'It happens that me and Lucy have a physical affinity. I have only to look at an object, for example a security card with a number on it, and as soon as I concentrate she can get it, read it straight out from my mind like reading a book. It's like I'm a broadcasting station and she's the receiver.'

It took a lot of swallowing. 'What's all this guff then about reading the future?'

He eyed me very solemnly. 'It's not guff, Hank. Occasionally Lucy receives a flash of foreknowledge and knows what the future holds.'

'Can she do it to order?'

His eyes seemed to burn into me with inspired fervour. 'If it's important enough. If she's allowed long enough to concentrate.'

Lucy had finished cleaning greasepaint from her face. She climbed to her feet, reached for a frothy under-garment draped over a chair. The slender silken strand around her loins fitted snugly enough to be her skin. It's wasn't any wider around back than it was in front!

She flashed me a dazzling smile that made the butterflies in my belly loop the loop, and said, 'Excuse me,' in a soft, haunting voice that made me sweat, and with perfect poise, like she was still on the stage, walked across to the screen, disappeared behind it.

I watched her all the way to the screen. Slim, long-legged and her body moving rhythmically. Her skin seemed so warm and full of life I could feel the heat of her from where I was sitting.

I was sweating!

'That's our real trouble,' gloomed Billy. 'Not enough publicity.'

It wasn't a high screen. I could see her head and then one dainty hand as she hung a black silken strand over the top of the screen.

'A dame like Lucy, with the power she possesses, linked to the right publicity, could really take us places,' he told me.

The other black silken strand, the one with the tiny, triangular section, appeared over the edge of the screen. I could picture her the way she was now, breathtakingly lovely, slim and taut, beautiful and perfectly proportioned. A pocket-Venus. And there was only that screen between us, only a fragile shield of silk defending her from my hot eyes!

'We need a boost,' said Billy. 'Just one good boost and we'll be made. Our name will spread like wildfire throughout the States.'

One bare arm showed above the screen, and then the other, as she threaded delicate, frothy under-scanties over her head. I figured Billy's wife must be really something if he could share a dressing-room with Lucy without growing even the slightest bit interested.

'Say,' he said, like he'd just thought of a bright idea. 'What was it you said you were doing?

Reporting? You've got a pull with newspaper men. How about it, Hank?'

'How about what?' I said hoarsely. I was watching the screen when she stepped out from behind it, hips and breasts ensnared in frothy feminine material that seemed to emphasise rather than conceal her points of interest. She glided back to her chair with the grace of a gazelle combined with the poise of a queen. The under-scanty was powder blue and semi-transparent. I could see the warm sheen of flesh through it.

'Every little helps, Hank,' Billy said excitedly. 'Just a line here or there, mentioning us, will help start folks taking a real interest. What about it, Hank? What d'you think of it, Lucy? Wouldn't it be fine if Hank could get us a little publicity.'

Her misty blue eyes came around to mine; soft, melting eyes, breathtaking and heady. 'That would be wonderful, Hank,' she breathed, so that suddenly I was sitting on air. As she spoke she kinda absentmindedly slipped her hand inside her bodice, gently, almost lovingly, moulded herself into position.

'Sure,' I croaked. 'I'll help if I can.'

She smiled gratefully, a smile that made me dizzy. I knew then that I wanted nothing more than the chance to date this dame and get to know her better – much better!

Billy said: 'We've got a coupla hours to spare before we're on again. What say we do the town together?'

That was when I remembered the cocktail party.

'I've gotta go,' I said desperately, climbing to my feet. My watch showed I was in danger of missing everything. I had to get at least a mention of the author into the *Chronicle*.

'Don't forget, Hank,' said Billy, extending his hand. 'Even just a line will help.'

'Sure, sure,' I said hurriedly. I was watching Lucy all the time, and her eyes were watching me too through the dressing-table mirror. 'Looking forward to seeing you soon,' she said invitingly.

Those blue eyes were an anaesthetic. I walked out of that dressing-room without touching the floor. I was still in a dream when I reached the cocktail party. And after I'd interviewed the literary lion my brain was still numbed with her beauty. I'd forgotten his name, had to ask a colleague who stared at me in astonishment like I was pulling his leg.*

---

* In the original edition of *Torment*, there appeared here the following 'Author's Note'. One can only speculate that the publisher must have had some kind of financial arrangement with the act referred to. Also of note is the fact that the publication date of *Torment* was wrongly suggested to be May 1953; it was actually April 1953:

Since writing this yarn I have met one of the partners of this act in London. The name of the act is changed but the act itself is the same. For those readers who may be interested to see this act and who live on the South Coast, I suggest you visit The City of Portsmouth Coronation Ideal Home and Trades Exhibition at Portsmouth. The name of the act is The Novellos, and the act opens on the 9th May 1953 and runs for three weeks until May 23rd, coinciding strangely enough with the month of publication of the book. HANK JANSON

2

Publicity can be double-edged. If it was useful to Billy it could also be useful to the *Chicago Chronicle*. After I'd spent a night figuring how to help Billy – or rather Lucy – I put my proposition to the Chief.

He was enthusiastic about it. It would give Billy and Lucy a boost and it would give the *Chronicle* a boost as well. A big boost, handled the right way.

I said nothing about it to Billy, attended the second performance of their show the following night, and was out of my seat, halfway on to the stage, almost before Billy began to invite observers to come forward from the audience.

They were good troupers. Not by so much as the flicker of an eyelash did Lucy or Billy show they knew me. Not that I worried. Standing maybe a coupla yards from Lucy while the fierce spotlight was on her was the kinda work I'd have liked to concentrate on for the rest of my life.

It was all too soon before Billy's act came to an end. And then the audience were treated to a surprise item. A surprise for Billy and Lucy too.

Earlier in the day, the Chief had been in touch with

the stage manager. The manager also liked the idea of publicity. He'd jumped at our suggestion. But Billy had been told nothing, and his eyes widened a fraction with conjecture when, instead of the curtain being run down, the manager came out on to the stage, took his stand before the microphone.

Even then, Lucy and Billy remained good troupers. Their faces registered only mild surprise.

The audience were silent, waiting and tense, sensing something unusual was about to take place.

The manager said evenly into the microphone:

'Tonight we have a special surprise item. Unknown to Los Guitanos, we have with us tonight a representative of the *Chicago Chronicle* who intends to challenge Los Guitanos. They claim their act to be the greatest miracle telepathy demonstration in the world. Quite independently, the *Chicago Chronicle* wishes to challenge this claim, put Los Guitanos to a severe test ...'

He paused, waited for the burst of applause to die away. I could sense excitement seething through the theatre. It wasn't altogether surprising. Everyone musta been asking themselves and wondering if this was a trick.

The manager said: 'I myself have no idea what form the test will take. But I have great pleasure in introducing now Mr Hank Janson, who is representing the *Chicago Chronicle* and in whose hands I now leave the reputation of Los Guitanos.'

There was a spatter of applause as I stepped forward to the microphone. My knees felt rubbery and my voice was dry. It was the first time I'd ever been on the stage and spoken to such a vast audience.

I said falteringly: 'On behalf of the *Chicago Chronicle*, I should first like to know if Los Guitanos are prepared to accept the challenge I am about to put to them?'

Billy immediately stepped up alongside me with an easy grace. His manner was full of confidence and charm. He said in his rich, convincing, baritone voice: 'Carmenita is a miracle girl. Her powers of telepathy phenomenal. Her ability to read minds and see the future transcends all material knowledge and science. We readily, no, eagerly, accept this challenge.'

Just for a moment his eyes caught mine. There was a gleam in them that seemed to say: *'Atta boy. Now you really are giving me a boost.'*

'Excellent,' I said. 'Now will somebody kindly hand the miracle girl a pencil and paper.'

Billy had pencil and paper in his pocket. He handed them to Lucy.

I waved everyone on the stage right away from Lucy, Billy included. I said slowly and deliberately: 'I wish you to listen to me very carefully. This is the challenge the *Chicago Chronicle* wishes to make. We wish you to write on that piece of paper, the banner headlines that will appear in next Saturday's issue of the *Chicago Chronicle.*'

There was a kinda united gasp from the audience. The observers up on the stage with me gaped, and the manager's eyebrows lifted. But Billy's face was expressionless.

'Now will you please write,' I said in a loud, ringing voice. 'Take your time, concentrate as long as you wish.'

I could feel the tenseness of the atmosphere so solid I could have cut it with a knife. The silence was thick and heavy. Every pair of eyes in the house was fastened on Lucy as she closed her eyes and concentrated.

The concentration continued, the silence continued, and Lucy continued concentrating.

A minute went past.

Two minutes. Three minutes. She was swaying perceptibly, like she was on the point of fainting. I could see Billy staring at her like he was willing her to do something. There were beads of perspiration rolling down his cheeks.

She concentrated so long and so hard, I was scared she'd never start writing and would maybe faint. Then with her eyes still closed she slowly moved her hands, pressed the point of the pencil to the paper, wrote on it slowly, laboriously.

When she finished writing she let her arms fall to her sides like she was exhausted.

'Everybody please stay exactly where they are,' I said in a loud, commanding voice.

Nobody moved.

I said clearly: 'Now will you please drop the pencil from your left hand and tear off the sheet of paper you have written upon.'

She did everything I directed very slowly, like she was drained of strength.

'Now fold the paper into four,' I instructed.

She did that, very slowly.

I had everything I needed in my pocket. I took the envelope and the two pieces of glass from my pocket, handed the pieces of glass around to the observers.

'I now wish everybody to witness very carefully what happens,' I said into the microphone. Slowly, and standing sideways so I would not obstruct the view of the audience, I advanced on Lucy, took the folded paper from her and slowly and carefully inserted it in the envelope. I then licked the flap of the envelope, fastened it down. I held the envelope high.

'I trust everyone in the audience is certain the words that have just been written are now enclosed in the envelope.'

The audience murmured agreement, the observers nodded their heads.

I passed the envelope to the two observers who had the pieces of glass. 'Will you kindly place the envelope between those two sheets of glass?'

The glass was cut just a little larger than the envelope.

I pulled blue ribbon from my pocket. 'Will someone else now tie this ribbon around the glass?'

They took a long time doing it, made a good job of it.

'Sealing wax,' I said, and produced it from my pocket. With matches they melted the wax, sealed the knots.

I said into the microphone: 'The ladies and gentlemen on the stage have witnessed every movement. I am now going to ask them if they are quite sure the message the miracle girl has written is now safely enclosed in the envelope and sealed between two pieces of glass?'

The observers all nodded vigorously.

I took a deep breath. 'Finally,' I said in a ringing voice, 'I am going to ask these observers to accompany me to the offices of the *Chicago Chronicle*. They themselves will carry the sealed envelope. The envelope will be placed in a prominent position in the office of the Editor throughout the day, and at night will be enclosed in the *Chicago Chronicle*'s safe. At noon on Saturday, in the presence of witnesses and reporters, the envelope will be opened and checked with the headlines of that day's *Chicago Chronicle.*'

I turned to Billy. 'Does everything meet with your approval, sir?'

Billy steeped forward to the microphone. He was bursting with confidence. He said in his rich voice: 'Ladies and gentlemen. The challenge just presented by the *Chicago Chronicle* presents no difficulties to the miracle girl. Carmenita has concentrated and looked into the future. She has seen what there is to be seen, and at twelve noon on Saturday, the miraculous powers of this girl will be made known to all.' He made a sweeping bow in reply to the wild burst of applause.

Everything went off better than I expected. There were ten observers, and we travelled together to the *Chicago Chronicle* in taxis. Not once did the envelope leave their hands. In a body, with *Chronicle* photographers flashlighting us, we walked through to the Chief's office.

There was a great deal of ceremony. The envelope was placed on a ledge immediately above the Chief's desk, where it could be seen by everyone in the office. Right beside it was the safe in which it would be locked up at nights when there was nobody around to see it.

Yeah, everything had gone off exceptionally well. Billy was gonna get all the publicity he needed, and the *Chicago Chronicle* was gonna benefit too. This was a stunt that was gonna interest everyone.

I felt happy for Billy as I checked through the proof of the story I'd written about the challenge and selected the photographs to be printed alongside it in the morning edition.

I got home late, happy that I'd done a good stroke of work, helped the *Chronicle* and Billy at the same time.

The telephone was ringing as I entered my apartment. I picked it up and Billy said down the line, with a note of relief: 'Thank heavens I've contacted you.'

'Went off pretty good, huh?' I said with satisfaction.

'I've gotta see you, Hank,' he panted. His voice was hoarse and he sounded desperate.

'Sure, Billy,' I said. 'I'll drop around tomorrow, sometime.'

'I've gotta see you right away,' he panted. 'It's urgent. Terribly urgent.'

'Can't it wait until tomorrow? I'm kinda all in now. Been working hard on giving you publicity,' I added happily, waiting for his gratitude.

'For Pete's sake, Hank,' he said desperately. 'Can you come on over to my hotel now? It's important. Terribly important.'

The worry in his voice got over to me. 'You want me to come *right* away?'

'You must, Hank,' he panted. 'You must.'

'Okay,' I sighed wearily. 'I'm on my way.'

I was thankful Billy was staying at a second-rate hotel tucked away in the suburbs. Even so, I was careful to keep my fedora pulled down low over my eyes and the collar of my slicker high up around my chin as I climbed the stairs to their room number. The challenge was on the level, but it wouldn't look good for me to be seen palsy-walsing with Billy after the *Chronicle* had issued the challenge.

Billy opened up directly I knuckled his door. He was wearing a dressing-gown, his hair was ruffled and there was a worried look in his eyes.

'What's on your mind?' I asked bluntly, skimming my fedora across the room so it fell on the bed.

He carefully locked the door behind me, crossed to the communicating door to the next room and knuckled it loudly. 'Are you there, Lucy?'

I heard her voice through the panels. 'Yes, I'm here.'

'I've got Hank with me,' he said thickly. 'We'd better talk.'

She drew back the bolts her side. Billy drew back the bolts on our side, and we pushed through into her bedroom.

Once again those misty blue eyes made me feel weightless, sent the butterflies crazily winging around inside me.

'I'm sorry there's only one chair,' she apologised. 'I hope you don't mind sitting on the bed.'

I didn't mind. I sat alongside her on the bed with enthusiasm, while Billy gloomily sank down into the chair. She was wearing a black silk dressing-gown, crossed over in front and tied with a girdle. I couldn't keep my eyes off her. I find dames wearing silk irresistible, on account silk is so fine and so clinging. Her robe was so fine and so clinging I would have staked my last dollar she wasn't wearing a stitch underneath it.

Billy said dismally: 'I've been kinda outta touch with things, Hank. I didn't realise you had so much pull with a big paper like the *Chicago Chronicle*.'

'It evens out,' I said. 'I didn't realise you had such a first-class act.'

'I'm worried,' he admitted. 'You've got me a lot of publicity.'

'I'm giving you a real boost,' I said cheerfully. I was watching Lucy, wondering why she should watch

Billy so devotedly and intently. After all, she was the mainstay of the act. She was the one who did the work. Billy just strung along, got places on account of her ability.

Billy said almost angrily: 'You shoulda talked it over with me first, Hank.'

'It went off sweetly,' I reminded him. 'Sweet and smooth. Impressive too. If I'd have mentioned it to you beforehand it may have seemed just the slightest bit phoney. As it is, everything went off perfectly.'

He scratched his unshaven jaw ruefully. Then he sighed. 'We had good bookings,' he said mournfully. 'We were booked in Chicago for another three weeks. Now we're all washed up.'

'Whad'ya talking about?' I demanded. 'All washed up? Why, this is the biggest thing you've ever done. This will put you on the front page of every newspaper in Chicago.'

'You're damned right,' he said, and his shoulders hunched dejectedly.

I stared at him. I'd been paying too much attention to Lucy. Only now was his manner beginning to have an impact on me. A cold feeling began to swell in my belly. I said, with growing understanding: 'Now wait a minute, Billy. What are you trying to tell me?'

His eyes came up, fixed mine, stared at me levelly. 'What's the chance of getting inside that envelope, Hank?' he asked bluntly.

I stared back at him. The cold swelling was as big as my belly, and my mouth was dry. 'You mean ...' I broke off, unable to finish the sentence.

He nodded stonily. 'Yep. We're all washed up in Chicago. We'll get our bags packed Friday night and catch the first train outta town Saturday morning. We're all washed up.'

I gaped. 'You're getting out of town?'

He climbed to his feet, paced up and down the room, scowling ferociously. 'The first time I've ever got this high on the billings, and now I'm all washed up. All on account I didn't use my head. All on account a guy tried to do me a favour.'

I said with my voice tinged with disbelief: 'You mean Lucy can't pull it off?'

'Pull it off?' he snarled. 'The way you've fixed it, we're gonna be the biggest laughing stock in show business.'

'But, wait a minute,' I protested. 'I asked you. You told me that sometimes she can see the future,' I gulped. 'You coulda cried off the Chicago Saturday headlines. We coulda stuck to telepathy, given her a stiff telepathy test.'

He glared at me. 'I'd rather have clairvoyance blown wide open than have our telepathy act broken.'

I glanced at Lucy, saw her troubled blue eyes still watching Billy intently. Then I looked back at Billy. I licked my lips nervously. 'Listen,' I said. 'You've gotta tell me. This telepathy … It's genuine, isn't it?'

He flung himself down in his chair, rested his elbows on his knees and his chin on his knuckles. He looked dispirited, unutterably weary and broken. 'It's an act,' he said mournfully. 'A system. It took three years to figure it out and train Lucy. It's one hundred percent stagecraft. Lucy couldn't read my mind any more than I can prophesy the six winning horses in tomorrow's races.'

'But you crazy dope,' I spluttered. 'I asked you beforehand and you told me. I asked you to put it on the line and …'

'Yeah, yeah, yeah,' he said, wearily. 'I told you it was genuine. But that's show business. You've gotta maintain the illusion. You've gotta convince everybody, even your best friends. Telepathy isn't like hypnotism. Hypnotism's possible. Telepathy is an act.'

I could see the spot I'd put them in. I'd given them a boost, a build-up. But it was a boost that was gonna kill them. It would laugh them out of the theatre, laugh them off the stage from one end of the States to the other.

'Jeepers, Billy,' I said contritely. 'If you'd levelled with me ...'

'Yeah, I know,' he said dully. 'It's all my fault. If I'd known you had so much pull with the *Chronicle* ...' He broke off, shrugged his shoulders.

Lucy said softly: 'I was scared, Billy. I didn't know what to write. I thought perhaps I should faint, and then realised that would be too suspicious.'

'You've gotta help us, Hank,' said Billy. 'Somehow that envelope's gotta get lost between now and Saturday. Your office has gotta catch fire or maybe get blown up. Somehow that envelope's gotta get lost.'

I looked at him levelly. 'There ain't a chance, Billy,' I said quietly. 'Even if I could do something, I wouldn't. There's more involved than just you and me and our friendship. It's the reputation of the *Chronicle* at stake. I can't risk that.'

He nodded understandingly. 'Sure, sure, sure,' he muttered. 'I just thought you might be able to do something. But I guessed that's the way it would be.'

'I can't think of a way out, Billy,' I told him miserably.

That seemed to be all there was to say. Through no fault of mine I had put them in a jam, and there was no way I could get them out of it.

Conversation flagged. Lucy's eyes seemed to have lost their mystical enchantment. I suddenly became acutely conscious they both wanted me the hell out of there.

I climbed to my feet. 'I'm sorry about this, Billy.'

'It's okay, Hank,' he said. 'It's okay.' He climbed to his feet, patted me on the shoulder. He sure knew how to take a bad break. But in his time he'd probably had plenty of experience of taking bad breaks.

I turned to Lucy. 'I hope we're gonna meet again sometime?'

She worked up a sad smile. 'I hope so,' she said. 'If we're here after Saturday, maybe we will. But until the envelope's opened it's wiser for us not to meet.'

I coulda taken her reply two ways. She coulda been stating facts or she coulda been dangling a carrot before my nose.

'Let's hope we meet after Saturday,' I said, without any hope at all.

She accompanied us to the communicating door, bolted it behind us.

'If you think of anything, Hank, let me know,' said Billy dismally.

'I can't, Billy,' I told him sincerely. 'I can't double-cross the *Chronicle*.'

'Sure, fella. I understand.' He worked up a smile, patted my shoulder. 'Come around again on Friday night anyway. Just to see the last of Los Guitanos.'

The memory of Lucy rode home in the cab with me. A wistful, sad memory. I felt like hell.

Imagine that; trying to do a guy a good turn and busting up his livelihood.

3

I was at police headquarters with my elbows on the counter, chatting to the desk sergeant and hinting I could do with a beer, when they brought him in.

Cop headquarters is one of the few places in Chicago you can buy liquor after four o'clock in the morning.

Two red-faced harness cops brought him in, heavy hands firmly grasping his shoulders and wrists like they thought he was an escapologist.

He was only a little guy. Each of those cops was four times his size, and the dismal way he drooped between them, shoulders hunched and jaw falling abjectly, made him look even smaller and more helpless.

They almost carried him over to the sergeant's desk, and I politely moved over, made way for them.

One of the bulls handed me a smarmed-up grin. He musta known who I was and figured he could use some publicity. 'My name's Mulligan,' he announced. 'Spelt with two l's.'

'I'll make a note of it,' I told him. I nodded at the little guy. 'Need any help with him?'

His skin was thicker than the soles of his boots. My

sarcasm made as much impression upon him as the once-over directed at a chorus girl.

'You don't have to worry, Mr Janson,' he said heartily. 'We can take care of this guy right enough.' His big fist tightened as he spoke, and the little guy's face creased in a silent whimper.

The desk sergeant pushed the papers on his desk to one side, opened a large, well-thumbed book, opened it at the last page and plunged a snub-nosed pen into a dirty inkwell.

'What d'ya want me to book him on?' he asked wearily.

'Attempted grave robbing,' said the cop.

I tipped my fedora to the back of my head with a forefinger, and fumbled in my breast pocket for my notebook.

The desk sergeant stopped sounding weary. His eyes lifted to the cop's, stared at him with an unspoken question, and then flicked to the mournful eyes of the little guy.

The little guy said, with a note of hopeless resignation in his voice: 'It's a frame. I didn't rob no graves. I didn't touch no graves.'

The desk sergeant said nothing, turned his gaze back to the book in front of him, laboriously began to write.

The scratching of the pen was loud. One of the cops was breathing heavily, wheezing like he had asthma. The desk sergeant finished what he was writing, blotted it very carefully.

'Name?' he asked tonelessly.

The little guy cleared his throat nervously. 'Joe,' he said. 'Joe Bates.'

The desk sergeant laboriously wrote the name. The

nib was crossed and spattered ink. The sergeant swore beneath his breath, blotted carefully like this was a work of art that would later be hung in a gallery.

There were other details he asked: address, age, and social security number. Finally he eyed the little man severely, said in a dull, metallic voice: 'You've heard the charge. Is there anything you wish to say?'

The little guy seemed to droop even lower. He opened his mouth, shut it, swallowed his Adam's apple a coupla times and then croaked: 'No. I guess there ain't nothin' to say.'

'All right, then. Let's see what you've got in your pockets.'

There was an interesting assortment in Joe Bates's pockets. A well-worn wallet containing greasy dollar bills, pieces of string, a pen-knife, a greasy envelope containing well-thumbed photographs, a copy of the *Chicago Chronicle* and a hip flask half-filled with brandy.

The bulls were disappointed. Maybe they'd been hoping he was carrying a set of housebreaking tools, or maybe a pick and shovel to give substance to their charge.

'Okay,' growled the desk sergeant. 'Give him his stuff back and put him away. The next sitting won't be for a coupla hours.' He pushed the envelope containing the photographs to one side. 'You don't get these back,' he said sternly, frowning at the little guy reprovingly.

The two cops guided Bates away, through the office, and down the steps at the far end.

I slipped my notebook back into my pocket, sighed regretfully. 'Doesn't sound like a story there.'

The desk sergeant shrugged his shoulders, nibbled the end of his pen. His eyes flicked down towards the envelope.

'How about buying me a pint,' I asked bluntly.

He strained around on his stool, stared up at the clock. 'I'll be off in twenty minutes. Want to wait until then?'

'I'm thirsty right now.'

Once again the eyes were straying towards the envelope. 'A thirst like that's valuable,' he said drily. 'Hold on to it. It improves with time.'

The two harness cops lumbered back into the office. Their broad faces wore the happy, contented expression of fellas who have done their duty well and are proud of themselves.

'I got your name right,' I told the one who had spoken to me. 'I'll spell it with two l's.'

'Fine,' he said. 'That's fine.' His chest swelled, and he looped his thumbs in the belt of his Sam Browne, like he was a cop who had rounded up twelve bank robbers single-handed.

'Suspected grave robbery,' I said slyly. 'Just how far down into the grave had he dug himself?'

The cop's chest swelled even more. 'He didn't get that far,' he said proudly. 'We caught him before he got started.'

'That means you've got nothing on him then? He wasn't digging, hadn't any tools?'

Mulligan glowered, and his beady eyes became resentful. 'We caught him, didn't we?' he demanded indignantly. 'Dodging around among the tombstones. Clear enough what he was after.'

'Think you can make the charge stick?'

The desk sergeant's straying fingers had worked open the flap of the envelope. He drew out the first photograph, stared at it intently.

The second cop reached out a fleshy hand, slid

another two photographs from the envelope.

My curiosity got the better of me. Me and Mulligan went for the last of the photographs together.

Joe Bates may have been preoccupied with death and spending his time dodging around tombstones. But his interest was in the living too. To put it more precisely, in the process that contributed to producing life.

I tossed the photograph back on the desk, disgust making my lips curl. For two people alone in a world of their own, that could have been something really special. But an intensely personal thing publicised in that ugly, blatant fashion turned my guts over.

Mulligan said with satisfaction: 'I could use a collection of these myself.'

The desk sergeant grunted, looked at the next photograph.

The second cop said with a leer: 'The judge may order them to be destroyed. Remember us. Don't be wasteful!'

I pulled my fedora down over my forehead, sauntered towards the door. Somehow I didn't want that drink any more. 'I'll be seeing you,' I grunted.

'Seeing ya,' grunted the sergeant without looking up.

Mulligan lifted his eyes momentarily. 'Don't forget,' he called after me. 'Spelt with two l's.'

'Sure,' I said.

As I pushed through into the street, I heard one of them tell the desk sergeant: 'That little guy's bellowing for his mouthpiece.' Then the door swung closed behind me.

I stood on the precinct steps, took a coupla deep breaths as I fumbled in my pocket for a cigarette, then lit up slowly. The street lamps threw yellow pools of light at intervals along the street, and immediately opposite across the road I saw a flicker of movement from a shadowy doorway.

I stood on the steps longer than I'd intended, watched the shadow intently, watched it for almost three minutes until it moved again. Then slowly, but with a kinda purposefulness, I walked down the steps, headed directly across the road.

That flushed the bird. She broke from cover like a rabbit flushed by a terrier, clip-clopped on frantic heels along the sidewalk, head down, arms swinging, walking as fast as she knew how.

Nothing of interest had happened all night. I was a reporter without a story, or even a lead to follow up. Nothing to occupy me except my curiosity.

I followed her.

Her high heels clattered tearfully on the concrete flagstones. I took long, solemn strides, timed three of her pattering paces to one of mine. That just about evened our speed.

In the yellow glare of the street lamps, I saw the white blob of her face as she glanced fearfully over her shoulder. Her pace quickened and she gained maybe a coupla yards before she tired.

I grinned to myself, consciously lengthened my stride and quickened my pace. The night air was bracing, and this was a rollicking, swinging pace I could maintain all night if necessary. It wasn't gonna be necessary, though. Already her footsteps were faltering, exhausted.

Steadily I gained on her, wearing her down, smiling as from time to time fear spurred her to a fresh effort so that for a few paces she widened the gap between us.

I stalked her relentlessly, walked her down with the grimness of a reporter with nothing else on his mind. And finally, as though realising flight was hopeless, she flattened herself against the wall, stared at me apprehensively as she waited for me to come abreast of her.

I slowed to a standstill, stood a coupla yards in front of her. The streetlights weren't so strong here, but I could see she was a young dame, a pretty dame, but a scared dame. I lifted the butt of my cigarette to my lips, drew on it until it glowed and red sparks were caught up in the night air. Then deliberately I flicked away the butt so it described a glowing arc into the gutter.

She stared at me fearfully, pressed back against the wall, panting so loudly I could almost hear her heart hammering too.

I let smoke dribble down my nose, then blew a plume of smoke towards her.

Throughout I didn't say a word.

She stared at me with a desperate, pathetic, panting fearfulness that reminded me of a stag that's been run to a standstill and is helplessly awaiting the baying hounds from which it no longer has the strength to flee.

Further along the street, the distant, mournful wail of a cat echoed across the tiles. Far away a distant cop siren pierced the night air. Nearby a clock chimed the quarter.

I stared at the girl and still said nothing.

She gasped, breathlessly, fearfully. 'What d'you want? I ain't done nothing.'

She was right of course. She hadn't done anything … except run.

'Why were you running?' I demanded bluntly.

She caught her breath. 'All right, copper,' she snarled. 'I'll tell you why I was running. Because I was scared. Scared of you following me.'

'You were spying on police headquarters,' I accused.

Her teeth clamped together, and her fear was slowly changing into resentment. Her eyes flashed bitterness.

'What were you watching for?' I demanded. 'What were you waiting for?'

'None of your business.' She was recovering her breath and her courage. She squared her shoulders. 'It's not a crime, is it? Looking at a police station?'

'No,' I said softly. 'It's not a crime. But it's kinda late for you to be out. Where d'ya live, kid? I'll walk you home.'

She shrank away from me, tried to force herself through the wall. 'Just keep away from me, copper,' she panted. 'Keep your dirty hands off me.'

I chuckled and watched her eyes narrow with suspicion.

'I'm not a cop,' I reassured her. 'Even if I was, I still wouldn't wanna harm you. It's late, kid. You didn't ought to be out alone.'

The sincerity in my voice was getting over to her. I could sense her softening up, see the suspicion in her eyes becoming dulled. 'You came out of there,' she whispered hoarsely. 'You followed me along the road and ...'

'I'm a reporter,' I said. 'I was in the station looking for a story. Now let me walk you a little way until we get a cab.'

She asked quickly, worriedly: 'Is that on the level, mister?' She gulped. 'You're not a cop?'

'On the level.'

She breathed a sigh of relief, kinda relaxed. Then suspicion tensed her all over once again. 'How do I know you're not lying?'

'Could be I am lying,' I said gently. 'There ain't no way of proving it.'

Her eyes were sharp with hostility. 'Why don't you leave me alone?'

'Listen, kid,' I said wearily. 'It's late. You're young to be out this time of night. Let me walk you home or get you a cab.'

'Not going home,' she said sullenly.

'Okay,' I said wearily. 'You're not going home. But you can't hang around the streets all night. Let me take you some place, buy you a coffee.'

She resented me, and yet she was in trouble and needed company to help her face the trouble. 'Why don't you leave me alone?' she asked again, but her voice was pleading with me to wear down her resistance.

'Come on, kid,' I said, my voice warm and encouraging. 'Let's get a warm cup of coffee.'

She stared at me resentfully but longingly. She said warily: 'No funny business?'

'Everything on the level.'

'Are you a cop or not?' she demanded.

'I'm not.'

She fought an internal battle. 'Where's the nearest place?' she asked grudgingly.

I nodded my head along the road. 'Ten minutes' walk,' I said. 'Let's go.'

She detached herself from the wall, eyeing me cautiously and careful to keep well away from me as we walked.

'I wish you'd leave me alone,' she grumbled.

'Sure, kid,' I agreed. 'I'll leave you alone. Let's have the coffee first.'

It was a cheerful, warm and brightly-lighted café. I steered her to the far end, where nobody could overhear us, and while we waited for the coffee, took my first good look at her.

She was maybe twenty-two, with dark hair and an oval, rather beautiful face that could easily become tragic. Her eyes dominated her face; large, brown, sad eyes that made it easy to forget her cheap jacket and skirt and the white blouse worn thin by frequent washing.

'You *are* a cop,' she breathed angrily. 'I can tell it, the way you're staring at me.'

'Climb down off the roundabout,' I said wearily. 'How does a guy prove he's not a cop, anyway?'

'He can't,' she said mournfully. Then her eyes lighted up. 'If you're a reporter, though, you can prove you're a reporter right enough. You're sure to have papers ...'

'Okay, kid,' I interrupted. 'If it's gonna take that mournful look outta your eyes, it's worthwhile.'

I pulled out my wallet, flashed my reporter's pass.

'Satisfied?' I demanded.

She sighed. 'I suppose so.' She still didn't sound happy.

A white-aproned waiter brought two thick coffee cups, set them down steaming beneath our nostrils.

'I get it,' I said. 'You don't like reporters either.'

'They work hand in glove with the cops,' she said dully.

I leaned forward across the table, stared into her eyes. 'All right, kid,' I encouraged. 'Come clean. You're scared of the cops and reporters. Who've you killed?'

She jerked back away from me, stared at me

distrustfully, then saw the smile flickering around my lips. 'You were only joking when you said that,' she accused dully.

'I'm not dumb,' I told her. 'I'm a guy who's been around. You're just a kid, and right now you're in trouble. I'd like to help you. Why don't you come clean?'

She stared down into her cup, stirred thoughtfully. Then, being careful not to look at me, she said guardedly: 'You were in the station for at least half an hour, weren't you?'

'Check.'

'You would have seen anyone brought in and charged?'

'Yeah,' I said. 'I was there waiting, hoping I might get a story and ...' I broke off abruptly, stared at her, willed her to raise her eyes to mine.

'So that's it,' I breathed. 'You were waiting outside for that little guy, that ...'

'Joe Bates,' she said dully.

'You were waiting for him?'

Her eyes went back to the coffee cup. She was still stirring mechanically. 'What did they charge him with?' Her voice was dead.

'Attempted grave robbery.'

She jerked upright, her eyes angry and hostile and then softening into perplexity. 'You're not joking?' she asked wonderingly. 'They're really charging him with that?'

'That's the way I heard it.'

Her forehead crinkled, and puzzlement was bright in her eyes. 'I don't understand,' she protested. 'Joe didn't do anything to be arrested for. All he did was climb over into the cemetery. There's nothing wrong about that, is there?'

'Depends,' I said reasonably. 'Depends on his intentions. Were you with him?'

'I tried to stop him,' she said. 'It seemed so silly. We'd been out to a party, and on the way back he suddenly said he'd get me some flowers, said he'd climb over into the cemetery and get them for me. Told me not to wait for him, to go on home and make coffee.'

'And you waited for him?' I guessed.

'What else could I do?' she asked miserably. 'It was such a crazy thing. In the middle of the night too. Then, when the police came, I hid in a doorway. Joe musta shown a light. They hid and waited for him, and when he climbed over the wall he dropped straight into their arms.'

'And you followed him to the police station?'

'It sounds crazy, doesn't it?' she said pleadingly.

'Yeah,' I said glumly. 'It sounds real crazy. But if it happened just the way you said, there's no reason for you to be so all-fired scared of cops.'

She looked down into her coffee, stirred it some more. 'Joe's been in trouble with the police before,' she admitted.

'Yeah,' I said sourly. 'I can imagine.'

She looked up quickly, pleadingly. 'But he's a good guy, really. I know he's been in trouble previously, stolen and gone to prison. But he's a good fella. He's got a good heart.'

Something had been worrying me all the time. I tried to work the worry out of my system. 'Just what does Joe Bates mean to you?'

She stirred her coffee more vigorously. 'He married my sister.'

From the way she spoke I could sense the drama behind those few simple words. Deliberately, calculatingly, I probed. 'But what does he mean to *you*?'

She still went on stirring. Pretty soon the milk in the coffee was gonna turn solid. 'Sis was twelve years older than me,' she said dully. 'When mother died, I went to live with Sis and Joe. He was a grand guy, as gentle as a lamb, looking after us the best he could. I guess he'd never have gone to jail if Sis hadn't been ill that time and needing special treatment. Joe had to get the money some way, and …'

'Your sister,' I said gently. 'Didn't she ought to know about Joe?'

I saw her fingers whiten as they tightened on the spoon. 'Sis died about a year ago,' she said in a choked voice. There was a pause like she was trying to swallow the lump in her throat. 'I kinda stayed on and helped look after Joe. He's kinda helpless by himself.'

'Drink your coffee, kid,' I said kindly.

Obediently she stopped stirring, lifted the cup to her lips, sipped at it slowly. Her eyes caught mine for a moment, and they were large and moist. Quickly she put down the cup, turned away from me, touched her forefinger to the corner of her eye. 'Excuse me,' she said in a choked voice. 'I'm being silly.'

'That's okay, kid,' I said gruffly. I caught the waiter's eye, beckoned him over, paid him off.

'Let's go,' I said.

She stared at me resentfully, suspiciously.

'Don't be a dope,' I growled. 'I'm taking you home. You can't go running around all night.'

'Joe …' she gulped. 'I've gotta do something about Joe.'

'Don't be stupid,' I said. 'There's nothing you can do for Joe now. He's asked for a lawyer to see him. His only real worry is you. I'll get in touch with him, tell him you're at home in bed. That will stop him worrying.'

Her wide eyes blinked at me through moist eyelashes. 'You'll really do that, tell him I'm all right?'

'Sure,' I said.

I ushered her to her feet and out into the night. I flagged her a cruising, late-night taxi and climbed in it with her, took her back to the tenement block in which she lived.

She didn't like it, but I escorted her up the stairs to the door of her apartment.

'Now don't worry, kid,' I told her. 'I'll get in touch with Joe, and if there's anything I can do, I'll help him.'

'Joe was crazy getting himself in a spot like this.'

'It'll sort itself out,' I said reassuringly. 'My guess is they haven't got enough on Joe to make their charge stick. Robbing graves is a big job, and Joe didn't have so much as a spoon on him to dig open a grave.'

She thrust the key in the lock, opened the door. 'You've been very kind,' she said.

'Just you go to bed and stop worrying.'

'I'd like to thank you for everything you've done,' she said. Her big eyes gazed up into mine earnestly. 'Shall I see you again?'

'We'll probably run into each other.'

'My name's Janice,' she said quickly. 'Janice Prescott.'

I couldn't sidestep that without it being obvious. 'Janson's my name,' I told her. '*Chicago Chronicle.*'

She gave me her hand, and her fingers were cool and firm. 'Thank you, Mr Janson,' she whispered, and kinda slipped inside and closed the door behind her before I realised she'd gone.

I glanced at my wrist watch in the flame of my cigarette lighter, fumbled my way downstairs and back to the waiting cab. My nightshift was almost over, and I was on duty again the following afternoon. I gave the driver the address of my apartment.

He was talkative for that early in the morning. 'Quickest goodnight I've ever known,' he commented through his mouthpiece.

'That's on account I've had a lot of practice,' I growled.

That slowed him down a bit. But not for long. A few moments later he said: 'You'd be surprised some of the things I see on this job, working nights.'

'I wouldn't,' I said drily. 'I've seen them myself.'

That slowed him down once more. He was still figuring out another angle of conversation when he cut across a red light and then stamped on his brakes, narrowly avoiding another taxi that veered away, missing us by the thickness of a skin of paint.

The driver lowered his window, spat through it disgustedly, angrily crashed his way up through the gears. 'D'you see that?' he demanded. 'A lunatic driver. Coulda killed us. Did you see it? A yellow cab!'

'Listen, bud,' I said grimly. 'The cabs in this town aren't yella. They'll attack anyone.'

That finished him. He never said another word except to tell me the amount of the cab fare when I reached my apartment.

4

It wasn't the biggest cemetery I've ever seen, and it certainly wasn't the most famous. But it was well laid-out, tastefully arranged and looking very much like a beautiful garden.

The outer walls were lined on the inside with closely-growing monkey-puzzle trees, and the uniformed guard at the entrance gate nodded to me genially as though I was an old friend.

Away over on my left, at the top of the hill and overlooking the forest of white headstones, was the church.

The uniformed attendant noted my indecision, eased himself from his chair and stepped out into the sunshine. 'Can I help you, mac? Got a grave number?'

'Yeah,' I said. 'A guy by the name of Williams. He runs this joint, I understand.'

He kinda drew himself up, his voice suddenly alert and respectful. 'You're visiting Mr Williams, sir?'

I nodded. 'That's right.'

'You turn off here to the right,' he told me, pointing. 'Straight down to the bottom of the hill, and take the path on the left signposted '*Superintendent*'. The road climbs, and when you get near the top, you'll see his house in the hollow on the other side.'

It was a long walk, but it was a pleasant day. There's an atmosphere of peace and serenity about a cemetery that makes a guy feel philosophical. I strolled along, listening to the silence and noticing how green the grass was beneath the sun, and even figuring what it was like being permanently resident in a joint like that, quiet and peaceful and away from the humdrum worries of life. Right then, in that cemetery, death seemed a peaceful, tranquil and restful termination to arduous living. We've all got to die someday. Death is the only thing in life that is certain. It comes to all of us, yet we're lucky because we don't think about death often. Only when death comes close, takes an unfair advantage and cuts a friend off in the midst of life – before they're ready to die – do we start thinking morbidly.

The superintendent's house couldn't have been better situated, dumped down in the midst of all that peacefulness and serenity, and surrounded by rose-covered trellises, cool fountains and goldfish ponds.

I pushed through a small wicker gate, threaded my way along a crazy paving, flanked by cool green lawns to the front door.

A thin, nervous and bespectacled young man opened the door, stared at me solemnly through large, horn-rimmed glassed. He wore a dark suit, a crisp white collar and a black tie.

'Mr Williams,' I said. 'Mr Preston Williams.'

He surveyed me doubtfully. 'Are you a detective?'

'No,' I said. 'But he'll see me.' I gave him my card. The one with *Chicago Chronicle* printed on it.

He was back in maybe two minutes, opening the door, ushering me along a corridor to a room labelled

'Superintendent's Office'.

The room was a blaze of sunlight, large windows overlooking the green lawns and the flower beds at the back of the house. Preston Williams came around from his desk, shook hands with me, waved his hand at his secretary in dismissal, and then settled himself down again in his swivel chair.

'I take it you've come about my wife,' he said directly.

I eased myself more comfortably in my chair, took a cigarette from the polished teak box he offered, and fumbled for my lighter. 'Yeah,' I said. 'It's about your wife.'

All the time, I was watching him, examining him, imprinting his mannerisms and features upon my mind. That's the way a reporter works.

He was a youngish guy, maybe thirty-five, with thinning black hair smarmed down like it was glued to his scalp with a fixative. His eyebrows were thin and his black eyes wide apart. He had a thin, pinched-in nose, which seemed all gristle, and his face was white and waxy so that the flush of his cheeks seemed unnatural, almost like rouge.

His black eyes were tragic as they stared at me across the desk. 'I do hope you have some news for me.'

I said bluntly: 'I don't wish to raise any false hopes, Mr Williams, so I'll tell you right away there's nothing new about your wife.'

He seemed to slump, his shoulders drooping and his eyes dropping from mine, staring unseeingly. Once again I was struck by the waxy pallor of his skin, the bloodlessness of his flesh and the almost artificially red spots on his cheeks. A revolting idea struck me. He looked like a stiff the undertakers had prepared for burial, colouring injected into the cheeks to make it life-like.

He said in a dead voice: 'The police? They haven't got anywhere, either?'

'You know better than me,' I told him. 'They're in direct communication with you, I imagine.'

He nodded slowly, numbly. 'I haven't heard from them for days.'

I cleared my throat, looked at the toes of my shoes. 'I hope this visit isn't upsetting you overmuch.'

His long, thin hand reached across the desk, picked up a paper knife, toyed with it mechanically. Again I was struck by the thinness and bloodlessness of his fingers. 'It doesn't matter about me,' he said hoarsely. 'Anything that helps to bring her back …' His voice broke off.

'I'd just like to check again,' I said. 'Your wife will have been missing three weeks tomorrow?'

He nodded dully. 'Not a trace of her,' he whispered.

'She left during the afternoon while you were supervising a burial at the church.'

He nodded mechanically.

'She left a note saying she would be visiting her sister and would be stopping over night.' I paused. 'Is that right?'

Again he nodded. His black eyes were far away, his long fingers nervous as they toyed with the paper knife.

'And because of that note, it wasn't until the following afternoon you became worried and began to make enquiries.'

'She hadn't been to her sister,' he said dully. 'She walked out of here that afternoon and hasn't been seen since.'

'Who saw her go?' I asked, sharply. 'Did anybody see her go?'

Those thin, bloodless fingers trembled and his tragic eyes climbed to mine. 'Nobody saw her go,' he whispered. 'It was the staff's afternoon off. Nobody was here. My secretary was with me up at the church.'

'And nobody on the staff lives in?'

Although his fingers were trembling and his black eyes were tragic, a ghost of a smile touched his lips. 'No staff ever seem to want to live in at a cemetery,' he breathed.

'Now tell me, Mr Williams,' I said directly. 'What do you really think has happened to your wife?'

He stared at me pathetically. 'Amnesia?' he said hopefully.

'The police have got her photograph. Her picture's been in every newspaper in this State. D'you think she'd have been missing for nearly three weeks without anyone seeing her?'

He licked his dry lips. 'I keep hoping,' he faltered. 'I keep hoping someone's going to see her, recognise her.'

'There is another possible explanation,' I said quietly, and didn't look at him.

The silence in the room was the silence of the grave. Seconds limped past on leaden feet. He said in a scared voice, so quietly I could hardly hear it: 'There can't be any possibility of ...' His words tailed off.

I was sweating. This was an uncomfortable job. 'Would there be anybody? I mean ... was there anyone who disliked her?'

'Nobody disliked her. Everybody liked her. The only thing is ...' His voice faltered away again.

I looked up sharply. 'The only thing is what?'

'Nothing,' he said quickly, and his fingers trembled quite openly as he toyed with the paper knife.

I took a deep breath. 'This is a serious matter, Mr Williams,' I said. 'Your wife has been missing a long while. So long there's cause to worry. So if you know anything, anything at all, no matter how personal, you owe it to your wife to mention it.'

It was like he was fighting a battle inside himself. 'I wouldn't want anyone to know this,' he said in a voice that was almost a whisper.

'If it isn't important, I shan't use it,' I told him. 'But if it helps to find your wife, the police and the press ought to know about it.'

'I certainly wouldn't want it in the papers,' he said, and there was a look of defiance in his eyes now.

'Okay. I won't print it. But maybe the police ought to know.'

'I'm not even sure about it,' he said mournfully.

'Sure about what?'

'I've had my suspicions a long while. Not strong suspicions. She was always so sweet, so gentle, I couldn't think of her doing anything … wrong!'

I began to see what he was driving at. 'You mean another man?' I asked bluntly.

His tragic eyes gleamed and his fingers shook. 'Little things,' he said. 'Nothing I could put my finger on. Nothing to really arouse my suspicion. Not until now, that is.' He took a deep breath. 'Looking back, I can remember the little lies, those times she went shopping and came back with nothing after a coupla hours. Little things like that, which didn't mean anything at the time, and probably don't mean anything now. Except … except it makes me think.'

'You've never heard of another guy, never heard a name mentioned, seen a letter, or anything like that?'

'I've looked through all her things,' he said tragically. 'There's nothing. Nothing at all.' He moistened his dry lips. 'Only ... if it was another man, she was very clever, kept it very secret.'

'Not even a telephone call?' I persisted. 'A man's voice, or perhaps a present that he gave her?'

He shook his head. 'Not a thing,' he said dully. 'Not a thing. It's just that after being married five years, a man gets to know his wife. It's nothing he can put his finger on, but he gets a feeling ... a strange kinda feeling.'

'How long you had this feeling?'

His eyes were wide as he stared at me. 'Since she's been gone,' he said hollowly. 'When I began to think back. It's like I told you, there's nothing to prove there's another man, and maybe I'm wrong anyway.'

We weren't getting anywhere fast. I climbed to my feet, rammed my fedora on the back of my head. 'I'm sorry about this, Mr Williams. I know it's been painful for you.'

'I don't mind,' he said hollowly. 'It doesn't matter about me. It's my wife. I just want to know she's safe. Even if she doesn't want to come back to me.'

'You can rely on the *Chronicle*,' I assured him. 'We'll keep plugging with her photograph. If she's around, sooner or later somebody's sure to see her and phone in.'

'I do so hope you'll have some success,' he said sincerely. 'Believe me, without Muriel, I'm completely lost.'

I could believe it, too. He looked like a guy who had passed through three weeks of hell.

Somehow the sun didn't seem to shine so brightly as I walked back to the gates of the cemetery. Somehow the attendant at the lodge gate seemed affected too. His nod of farewell when I bade him good-day was almost morose.

But maybe that was on account I didn't give him a tip.

I sat across the desk from Detective Inspector Blunt and stared back challengingly into his steel grey eyes.

'No, Hank,' he said. 'We're not making any official statement.'

'But you've got to say something,' I persisted. 'The dame's been missing nearly three weeks. I've just come from her husband, and there isn't one extra fact he can give us. She just walked out and disappeared.'

'Okay,' he growled. 'So we're looking for her. What else can we do?'

'Make it first-class priority,' I said. 'Suspected foul play. Turn out all the cops to find her body.'

His grey eyes drilled into the heart of my brains. He said softly: 'Where d'you get that foul play stuff from, Janson? Who said anything about foul play?'

'She's missing, ain't she?'

'Yeah,' he agreed. 'But so are fifty thousand other folk in this State. The number of folk who walk out of their homes and are never seen again would make an army big enough to win a war. But when someone goes missing on account they're murdered, they don't stay missing long. Because a body ain't the kinda thing that can keep itself out of sight. Sooner or later, someone's sure to stumble on it.'

'Okay,' I said disconsolately. 'So I haven't got a

story.'

He said quietly: 'What made you think of foul play, Janson?'

'Well, it could be, couldn't it?' I defended.

He stared at me for such a long time, I wriggled uncomfortably in my chair. He said finally: 'Don't go off half-cock on this, Janson. You might cut straight across police policy.'

I was completely in the dark as to what he was getting at. But I switched a know-all expression on to my face, leaned forward across the desk, tapped on it with my forefinger. 'Okay,' I said. 'What's your proposition?'

He took a deep breath, a very deep breath. 'I don't know how much you know, Janson, but I'm warning you to play this close to your chest. Any cheap, capital-making publicity you hand out may be a boomerang.'

'I'll make a deal,' I said crisply. 'Tell me all you know, and I'll tell you all I know, and in addition I'll promise not to print a word until I receive your okay.'

He kept staring at me so long I thought he wasn't gonna reply at all. Then he said with a strange note in his voice: 'Okay, Janson. It's a deal.'

'A deal!' I agreed.

A slow smile spread across his face. 'You missed out this time, Hank,' he said. 'Because our department knows very little. This time you've pulled a boner.'

'I'm listening,' I told him. 'I'm all ears.'

'It's brief and to the point,' he grinned. 'The information's available for anyone who takes the trouble to check up.' His eyes watched mine expectantly.

I said nothing.

He shrugged his shoulders, continued: 'Muriel Wood and Williams married five years ago,' he said, like he was reading an official report. 'As you know, he's the superintendent of the cemetery. Not everybody's idea of an ideal job. Not a particularly well-paid job either. But he's comfortable, house thrown in, together with a salary that takes care of any normal guy's wants.'

'Is any guy ever satisfied?' I asked.

He ignored me. 'Williams's wife was an orphan and worked as a shop assistant. When they married, her savings, after she had bought her trousseau, totalled exactly five dollars and seventy-five cents. That information's straight from her bank manager.'

'Unusual dame,' I commented.

'Unusual?' His eyebrows arched enquiringly.

'Couldn't think of anything to spend five dollars and seventy-five cents on,' I explained.

He cleared his throat reprimandingly. 'Married life was uneventful for the first year,' he said. 'Then, when they'd been married almost a year, a solicitor from way out West contacted Muriel Wood, informed her a long-lost relative who made a fortune out of oil had kicked off and left her a fortune.'

'A fortune!' I echoed.

'Maybe you don't think so highly of two hundred grand,' he said drily.

'Two hundred grand!' I gasped. The amount made me dizzy. Only figuring out how to spend that much dough would be the work of a lifetime.

'Just a minute,' I said breathlessly. 'You mean Williams and his wife have got all that dough, yet he's still working as a superintendent?'

His voice was dry. 'Muriel Wood was a very level-headed girl,' he went on. 'She invested the money wisely, was careful to see Williams drew only an agreed percentage of the interest received.'

'Something screwy about that,' I said. 'A man and

wife are a partnership. They share things equally and ...'

'It seems,' he interrupted heavily, 'that in his early youth, Williams was something of a gambler. Even before they came into money, there had been continual difficulty over a period of time because Williams lost more at cards at his club than his job could afford.'

'But hang on ...' I began.

His grey eyes were surprised. 'I thought you'd been around, Hank. Can't you see the way it was, his wife getting hold of money and using it as a lever? Every time Williams stepped out of line, got a little drunk or gambled too much or arrived home late, his wife pulled the purse strings together.'

Blunt had something there. 'Yeah,' I admitted, 'I can see the way it could be.'

He hooked his long legs under the desk, tilted back his chair and looked up at the ceiling. He said casually: 'Now if this business should prove to be foul play, as you suggest, what is the first thing you'd look for?'

'What's this, a quiz?'

'You'd look for a motive, wouldn't you, Hank?' he said gently. 'A nice, big, juicy motive.'

I saw what he was driving at. 'Like a two hundred grand motive?'

'That's right, sonny,' he said kindly. 'You've won yourself a coconut. And if Muriel Williams turns up dead, Preston Williams has won himself two hundred grand.'

'There's a will?'

'Sure,' he said, with satisfaction. 'There's a will right enough. All of it, every penny of it, every stock and bond, goes to Williams. Two hundred grand with interest!'

'So you figure Williams killed his wife?' I asked

bluntly.

Blunt's grey eyes came down from the ceiling, stared at me solemnly. 'Did I say that?'

'I'm asking you.'

He brought his chair back to even keel, leaned forward with his elbows on the desk and made a tent with his fingers. 'That's all I know, Janson,' he said. 'Williams's wife disappeared and I told you the background. I haven't one shred of evidence against Williams, not one witness, not one whisper of suspicion. But I've been in police business a long time. If Muriel Williams turns up dead, I'm not going to have to go far to start looking for a suspect.'

'And if she don't turn up?'

'Then Williams doesn't get the two hundred grand,' he said with satisfaction.

'You seen Williams?' I asked directly.

'Sure, that's part of my business.'

'How did he strike you?'

'A very worried man,' he told me.

'Wouldn't any guy be?' I demanded. 'Especially when his wife's holding the purse strings?'

'Maybe you know where we can find his wife,' he said sarcastically.

'A guy with all that dough willed to him, ain't gonna be so crazy he'll bump off his wife,' I said with conviction. 'The motive sticks out a mile. It's such a strong motive, even an innocent husband could easily find himself in the chair for suspicion alone.'

Blunt glared. 'Cut that, Janson,' he snapped. 'When we fry a guy, we don't make mistakes. We're sure. We're good and sure.'

'I hope so,' I said sincerely.

There was an awkward silence. He said abruptly:

'Now it's up to you. I've told you all the department knows. Now you can start in telling me what you've turned up.'

I grinned at him brightly. 'I've turned up exactly nothing, Blunt. To me this isn't anything more than the case of a missing dame. I never even checked up on the background. But thanks for the information. It will save me time and trouble.'

Blunt glared. 'You mean you came in here, making suggestions and dropping veiled hints without having anything to work on?'

I sighed. 'Listen,' I said wearily. 'I'm a leg man, a reporter. I get ten cents for every word I write and a bonus. If there's no story, I can't write. If I don't write, there's nothing to print. If there's nothing to print, the *Chicago Chronicle* loses circulation. And if the paper loses circulation, it goes bust. Then what happens?'

'You starve,' he said hopefully.

'It doesn't ever happen,' I said. 'I dig up a story, somehow, someplace, sometime.'

'Give me a new angle on Williams's missing wife and I'll pay you ten cents a word myself,' he offered.

I reached for my hat. 'I won't take you up on it,' I told him. 'I've got a hunch that some time Mrs Muriel Williams is gonna come bursting into the limelight and leave you with a whole bunch of murder motives to hang around another innocent fella's neck.'

'Listen, Janson,' he snarled. 'I don't like those cracks about innocent guys. I could get mad.'

'I can imagine,' I said bitterly. 'It's sure interesting to see the way you guys work. Nobody's been murdered yet, but already you've got a guy lined up, good and ready for the chair.'

He took a deep breath. Then he allowed air to

slowly escape from his lips, and I could almost sense him counting. He said quietly, surprisingly quietly: 'Take it easy, Hank. Take it easy, will you? You're going around the bend on that line. I know we got out of step and had Frank Baker lined up on a murder charge when he was innocent; but we straightened that out'*

'You had him all lined up right enough,' I gritted. 'You'd have strapped him in the chair and thrown the switch too. You'd have taken an innocent guy, built up evidence against him, burned him with voltage until his twisted, burned out body was dead. Deader than the grave.'

His lips were pressed tightly together as he fought to keep calm. He said earnestly, urgently: 'You've got to listen to me, Hank. You're going round the bend on it, I tell you. It's like I've said. We never fry a guy until we're sure. Absolutely sure.'

Maybe he was right. Maybe I *was* going around the bend. The surge of angry, hot blood lapping at the base of my brain was turning everything around me red. But his calm, dispassionate voice was gentle, soothing, calming and strangely pleasant. Yeah, maybe when a thing's close to you, real close, you get a slant that's off beam. I've known Blunt a long time. He's always been a good guy. A good cop. You have to be grateful for good cops.

I climbed to my feet. 'Skip it,' I said.

There was a hint of worry in his grey eyes. 'You've

---

* The original edition of "Torment" included here the following footnote:

Frank Butler was an innocent guy, framed and charged with murder. For those who want to read this yarn, ask your bookseller for "Suspense" by HANK JANSON.

got to get it out of your system, Hank,' he said. 'It coulda happened that way to anyone. It's just that much worse because it happened to somebody you know.'

'Yeah,' I said dully. 'I guess so.' I walked towards the door, turned to face him as I grasped the door-handle.

'Forget it, will ya, Blunt,' I growled.

There was a soft note in his voice now. 'Sure, Hank,' he said. 'I'll forget it.' He added as a kinda parting shot: 'If you dig up an interesting story, let me in on it, will ya? Maybe I can arrest somebody.'

5

I hadn't been back in the office more than half an hour when our freckled-faced office boy came up to my desk using a leer big enough to wear his clothes.

'What you been up to?' I demanded.

'I've been smart,' he said. 'I'm clean. It's you she's asking for.'

'Who?'

'A dame named Prescott.'

The name clicked through my mental filing cabinet, slipped into position beneath the mental picture of a young dame with an oval face. Linked to her was a little guy named Joe Bates who chased around graveyards with glossy photographs in his pocket.

'Where is she?'

'In the waiting-room.'

'Okay,' I grunted. 'I'll see her in a minute.'

She looked even smaller, sadder and more pathetic than I remembered when I pushed into the waiting room maybe five minutes later. She climbed to her feet quickly, and her eyes were moist.

'I had to see you,' she said earnestly.

'Sure, sure,' I said, and my eyes went over her

shoulder to the short, sturdy guy standing behind her. He was young too, maybe a year older than her. He had curly red hair, blue eyes and an aggressively jutting chin spangled with freckles.

She was flustered. 'I hope you don't mind, Mr Janson. But Red, he's my boyfriend, he was with me and …'

'Hiya, Red,' I said.

'Hiya, Mr Janson,' he said, and flushed uncomfortably, shuffled his feet nervously.

'Take it easy,' I said. 'Park the bodies.' I hitched one thigh onto the table and offered them cigarettes. Both of them perched on the edges on the edges of chairs like they thought they might explode. Both solemnly refused to smoke.

'Well, what's on your mind, kid?' I asked.

'It's Joe,' she said worriedly. 'I thought everything was going to be all right and now … now …' her voice broke and the tears looked like they might break loose any minute.

'Now don't upset yourself,' I said soothingly. 'Just tell me the trouble.'

Red said fiercely: 'They've sent Joe to jail.'

'What!'

'Seven days,' gulped Janice. 'Didn't even let me see him. Sent him straight off to prison.'

'That's crazy,' I said. 'They can't jail a guy for wandering around a cemetery.'

Red said fiercely: 'It was the photographs they charged him with. Dirty photographs. They gave him seven days.'

That was a new angle. So the cops had dropped the graveyard charge and brought a charge for circulating photographs. That was tough.

'It's not true,' said Janice earnestly. 'They didn't belong to Joe. He found them in the churchyard. All he did was pick up the envelope and put them in his pocket. He didn't even know what was inside.'

'That's why we've come to see you,' said Red. 'We know you help guys who are in trouble when it's not their fault. So I thought … Janice thought … maybe you can do something for Joe. Because those photographs weren't his. Understand?' He gulped. 'Joe found them.'

'Yeah, I understand,' I said bleakly. Naturally enough, Joe wasn't going to admit to his wife's kid sister he carried those kinda photographs around in his pocket.

Her wide eyes were looking at me beseechingly. 'So you will do something to help Joe, won't you, Mr Janson?'

What could I say?

Could I tell her I wouldn't help or couldn't help? Should I tell her that Joe was probably guilty anyway? Should I destroy her faith in Joe, tell her what I really thought?

I did what any other guy would have done. I strung her along. I only needed to string her along for a few days and then Joe would be out of jail, solving the problem.

'I'll look into it, kid.'

'You will?' she said happily, excitedly.

'Yeah,' I said. 'I'll phone a coupla mouthpieces, get their opinion.'

'You're so kind,' she said, eyes sparkling with thankfulness.

I flushed. I knew I was a heel. A ripe, low-down heel. The way Red was looking at me with just the slightest hint of suspicion in his eyes didn't make me feel any happier.

'How soon d'you think you'll know something?' she asked eagerly.

'That's difficult,' I said. 'Write your name and address for me and I'll get in touch with you.'

Happily, almost contentedly, she wrote her address for me.

I took the slip of paper from her, folded it and placed it in my waistcoat pocket. 'Anything else, kids?'

'What more could you do for us?' she asked sincerely.

I couldn't meet her eyes. I turned, made towards the door. Then I suddenly remembered Joe was the breadwinner and she was just a kid. I turned back, my hand going into my breast-pocket. 'How are you fixed, kid?' I asked. I opened up my wallet, counted off the bucks. 'Maybe you'll take a little gift just to help you along until Joe gets home.'

Red shouldered forward, his head low and his shoulders hunched aggressively. He said menacingly: 'Just a minute, mister. That's my girl you're offering dough.'

I liked his spirit, but couldn't stop myself from grinning. 'Hold your horses, kid. I'm not making improper suggestions.'

'Don't be silly, Red,' she snapped. 'How dare you speak to Mr Janson that way.' She took his arm, tugged on it ineffectually.

He jutted his jaw obstinately. 'You was offering her money,' he accused doggedly.

I sighed wearily. 'Does it make any difference if I make her a loan?'

'No,' he gritted. 'It doesn't make any difference.'

'Don't be crazy, Red,' she reproved, really annoyed

with him. She tugged his arm, shook him in anger.

'Be sensible,' I told him. 'Who's gonna take care of her until Joe gets out?'

'I will,' he said pugnaciously. 'Janice didn't come here expecting money or loans. So start putting that billfold back in your pocket.'

The guy had spunk, and I had a sneaking admiration for him. But he was too young to be getting so goddamned serious. I shrugged unhappily, replaced the billfold in my pocket 'If you do hit trouble, kid,' I told Janice, 'you still know where to come to get help.'

'She's taking no money from no-one,' he grated ominously.

'Aw, Red! Why d'you have to act this way?'

'I don't think anyone's gonna have to worry about you, Janice,' I told her. 'Red's gonna look after you swell.'

I turned to the door, opened it, whistled for the office boy. 'Show my two visitors out, will you?' I instructed, and shook hands with them, escaped as quickly as possible. I had a guilty feeling, knew I was being a heel. Because I wasn't gonna ring any mouthpiece. I wasn't gonna ring anybody. There was just nothing I could do. Joe Bates would have to serve his time.

Maybe half an hour later, the office boy was leering at me again. 'What is it this time?' I growled.

'Same thing,' he grinned. 'A dame.'

I sighed. 'Same dame?'

'Different dame.'

'What she want?'

'Won't say,' he said. 'Won't talk to anybody but you. Won't say what she wants. Insists on seeing you.'

Even though a guy's a reporter, he still has certain

rights and privileges.

'Tell her I won't see her unless she gives her name and her business.'

He was back within ten minutes, wearing the biggest leer I'd seen to date. 'Boy, is she sold on you. Won't give her name or business to anyone but you. Pretty as hell but stubborn as a mule. Guess you'll have to climb down, because she won't budge.'

'Listen,' I said evenly. 'You go right back, tell her she can sit there until doomsday unless she gives me her name and her business.'

'I've told her that,' he said laconically.

'Then tell her again.'

'Okay,' he said. 'You're the boss.' He walked off whistling, even his shoulders and the way he walked seeming to leer at me.

Twenty minutes later he hadn't come back. That little itch of curiosity, which is an essential part of my make-up, was at work. I picked up the telephone, had myself put through to his department. 'That you, Freckles?'

'That's right,' he agreed.

'What's happened to that dame?'

'I told you,' he said in a pained voice. 'She's obstinate. She's got her fanny glued to that chair and, like you said, she's there until doomsday.'

'A dame that stupid just ain't worth bothering with,' I grunted. 'Let her go on waiting until she gets tired.'

Another twenty minutes passed. I found myself wondering what she was like, why it was me she insisted on seeing. I wondered if I knew her.

The tiny itch of curiosity grew and grew and grew.

I found I had to see Jones the accountant on a

matter of expenses, descended to the first floor, passed by the door of the waiting-room.

Ten minutes later, when I'd settled the little accountancy problem, I passed the door of the waiting-room a second time.

I just had to know if she was still waiting.

I pushed open the door of the room, looked inside, apologised quickly, and closed the door again.

I'd had a split second glimpse of the dame. She wasn't anyone I knew. I hadn't seen her before. But there was enough of her showing above the rim of her magazine to prove Freckles hadn't made any overstatement. She sure was pretty. As pretty as hell.

I went back to my desk, picked up the phone, got through to Freckles.

'Listen,' I said. 'That dame still waiting?'

Somehow he managed to send a leer along the line. 'You should know. You just ducked in to peek at her.'

I flushed. 'Give her an ultimatum,' I said. 'Five minutes to state her name and business or else she goes out. Understand? She goes out. She can't wait here. Get it?'

'Why do you have to say everything three times?'

'You just do what I tell you,' I growled, 'and quick.'

I hung up, blue-pencilled editorial copy, and all the time curiosity was itching inside me. At the end of a quarter of an hour, I couldn't control my curiosity any longer. Once again I telephoned Freckles. 'What about that dame?' I growled.

'What about her?' he retorted.

'Did you do what I told you?'

'Sure,' he said.

'All right,' I said, exasperated. 'Tell me. What

happened? What did she say?'

'Nothing,' he said laconically. 'She didn't say a thing.'

'Did you tell her she'd have to leave?'

'Sure.'

'Well, if she won't talk, make her leave.'

'I don't have to,' he said. 'She's already left.'

Freckles was maybe eighteen. When he grew up he was gonna be a real smart kid. He was having himself a whale of a time dangling me on a piece of string.

'You're sure she's left?' I demanded. She had been waiting so long, I couldn't imagine her leaving that easy.

'Sure I'm sure,' he said. 'I escorted her from the premises myself.'

He still had that leer in his voice. There was something more too. A kinda mocking note like he knew something I didn't.

'And she didn't give her name?' I persisted.

'She didn't give nothing. And remember, any time you have another dame you want me to give the bum rush, just call on me.'

That itch of curiosity was at work inside me, nibbling away at my brain all the time I was blue-pencilling. I'd have been crazy to interview that dame without knowing who she was or what she wanted. A guy can get himself into all kinds of trouble that way.

But I couldn't get her out of my mind, remembering that fleeting glimpse of her, wondering what her name was, wondering why she particularly wanted to see me and why she wouldn't see anyone else.

I was still wondering about her when I cleared my desk for the night, reached for my fedora, nodded to the others as I strolled out through the newsroom and along the corridor to the elevator.

Outside it was almost dusk. I walked around back of the office to the parking lot, threaded my way through the cars and brought up against my own car.

There was somebody sitting inside.

I opened the door, said sharply: 'Excuse me, miss. You musta made a mistake.'

'I haven't made a mistake,' she said. She spoke quietly, her voice clear, almost bell-like.

I took a second gander and recognised her.

I took a deep breath. 'You're awful persistent.'

'Climb in and sit down,' she invited. 'I won't bite.'

'You're pretty sure of yourself.'

'Am I?' she said thoughtfully. 'I wonder!'

'Why won't you give your name and say what you want?'

'You are Hank Janson, aren't you?' she countered. A cigarette lighter flared momentarily. 'Yes,' she said with satisfaction. 'I'm really talking to you at last.'

Her calm assurance got me rattled. It was like she'd taken over control, placed a firm hand on the reins, and was herding me in the direction she wanted to go. Instinctively I chafed at the bit. 'I'm off duty,' I told her. 'If you wanna see me you can call at my office tomorrow, state your name and your business.'

She chuckled, a friendly, musical chuckle. 'Just how obstinate can you get?'

'Me! Obstinate!' I echoed.

'Climb in and make yourself comfortable so we can talk,' she invited a second time.

Again I tried to spit the bit out from between my teeth. 'This car's private property,' I pointed out. 'You've no business to be sitting in this car.'

'All right,' she agreed placidly. 'I've no right to be sitting in the car. What happens now?'

'I call the cops,' I said grimly.

She shrugged her shoulders forlornly. 'You really do intend to be tiresome, don't you?'

'You want I should call the cops?' I asked darkly.

'Of course I don't.' She shrugged her shoulders again. 'But if that's the way you feel, I guess there's nothing I can do about it.'

'You can climb out and let me go home ... alone.'

'Why don't you be a good fella?' she pleaded. 'All I want is a chance to have a quiet talk with you.'

'I'll count to three and then I'll call the cops,' I threatened. 'You know what that means. You'll be taken down headquarters.'

'I wouldn't like that,' she said anxiously.

'One,' I counted.

She settled back in the seat, folded her arms. 'I wish you'd tell me what I've done wrong. Have I gone about this the wrong way?'

'Two,' I said grimly.

'Because I don't see how I can tell this to anybody else.'

'Three,' I said.

She sighed. 'Okay,' she said. 'Get the cops. Maybe you'll feel better afterwards.'

She wasn't gonna move.

If I was gonna get a cop, she was gonna sit right there and wait for him. I hesitated, standing there holding the door. I could see the whites of her eyes shining through the darkness. Then it was my turn to sigh. 'Okay,' I conceded. 'I'll save you from the cops.' I slid behind the driving wheel, slammed the door.

'Whew. I really thought you'd get a cop.'

'If I had, what would you have done?'

'Sat here and waited.'

'Just what I figured. Does that make you crazy?'

'Maybe,' she said thoughtfully. 'But if it was the way to get you listening to me, I had to do it that way.'

'What's on your mind, then?'

'There's a whole lot on my mind, and it's gonna take a long while to tell you.'

'Why pick on me?'

'Because I know about you. Because I've read your stuff. Because I feel you're the one guy maybe who can help me.'

I groaned. 'Why me? There's two hundred million other guys in the States.'

'Aren't you flattered?'

'Listen, sister,' I growled. 'It's only adolescents who get flattered. Kids of eighteen and nineteen.'

'Okay,' she said. 'So you're a grown-up guy. A real big boy. So if I can't flatter you, how else can I appeal to you?'

'Look,' I said. 'You've got a problem or something. You think I can help out on it. Maybe I can't. So tell me what it is, briefly, and I'll answer you right away.'

'It's a big problem,' she said. 'It'll take a long while to outline.'

Again I groaned. 'You wanna make a meal of it.'

'That's not a bad idea,' she said quickly.

I said drily: 'I wasn't issuing invitations to dinner. I was suggesting you wanna take time outlining the problem.'

'It's still not a bad idea,' she said thoughtfully. 'I could talk while we're having dinner.' She flashed me a sidelong glance. 'The dinner's on me, of course.'

I turned the ignition key, thumbed the starter button, trod gas as the engine turned over.

'All right,' I said wearily. 'I give up fighting.

You're gonna get your way.'

'It's so nice of you, Mr Janson,' she said softly. 'You're so kind.'

'Yeah,' I gritted darkly.

'You've been so charming about it all.' The sweetness of her voice only thinly coated the bitterness of contempt.

6

She wasn't a talkative dame; she sat wrapped up in her own thoughts while I drove to an eating house I knew out on the South Bend.

She was a dame with character and a mind of her own as well as a grim determination. Yet there was something more; a kinda tragic relentlessness about her that I sensed and that made me uncomfortable. It wasn't until she was sitting opposite me, after the waiter had taken our order, that I asked: 'What's your name?'

'Betty Scott,' she said dully.

'Okay, Betty,' I grinned. 'Since we're gonna have dinner together, we may as well try to make it pleasant. I'm willing to thaw, listen to your problem.'

'And have I got problems!' she said. For the first time, her brown eyes met mine, stared at me levelly.

I hadn't really got a square look at her until now. She was worth looking at. She wasn't exactly pretty, but she was plenty attractive.

She had one of those haughty kinda faces that can be beautiful or disdainful or, when the owner wishes, softly tender and charming. Right now there were the shadows of worry beneath her eyes and a hint of hope as she stared at me.

'I'm looking for a man,' she said simply.

'So are most dames,' I said. 'That's what makes it so tough for a guy to be a bachelor.'

She wasn't amused. 'His name is John Maitland,' she said simply. 'He's tall, over six feet, very dark, jet black hair. He wears a moustache and a small, pointed beard. He *was* living in Clinton.'

'A guy like that shouldn't be hard to find if you have his address.'

Her voice was hollow. 'Just over a few weeks ago, he came to Chicago. I've visited all the clubs and hotels he was supposed to frequent. They've never heard of him.'

I gave her an up-and-under look. 'Jilted?' I guessed.

Her eyes were suddenly hard and bitter. 'I've never met him,' she gritted. Her small hands resting on the table in front of her clenched until white bone gleamed through her skin. 'I want to meet him,' she breathed. 'I want to meet him ... just once!'

The waiter brought the soup. I shook out my napkin, spread it on my lap, watched her surreptitiously as she used her napkin. She was getting me interested. Not only on account of her problem, which didn't seem such a helluva problem at that. But because of herself. She sure was a dame with character. The kinda dame a fella like me could find interesting enough to string along with.

Between mouthfuls of soup, I asked: 'Any special reason why you want to meet this John Maitland?'

Her eyes glittered. 'Yes,' she said, and it was some seconds before her suddenly mean voice could be got under control and permit her to continue.

'I had a kid sister,' she gulped. 'A kid sister just turned seventeen. Since our folks died, I've been looking after her. But Pat had a mind of her own. She accepted an office job in Clinton, a coupla hundred miles from home. I couldn't stop her from going.'

I was beginning to cotton on. 'It was your sister who knew John Maitland?'

She nodded. 'Pat always told me everything. She wrote to me every day. She told me about him, how she had met him and how very much in love with him she was. She wrote me everything about him. I figured she was sensible enough to look after herself, didn't worry until she wrote and told me ...' She broke off.

I could guess. 'Pregnant?'

She nodded silently, kinda choked.

'And the guy wouldn't marry her?'

'He said he *would* marry her,' said Betty. 'That made Pat happy. Every letter I got from her after that was happy and excited, full of plans for the forthcoming marriage, promising to bring John to see me when they took their honeymoon. I was worried about Pat, but I couldn't be unhappy, because she was obviously so happy. Reading her letters made me envy her. It wasn't right for any girl to be as happy as Pat was.'

I said nothing, watched her hands nervously clenching and unclenching.

'Then he left Pat,' she said simply.

There was nothing shocking about her story. It had happened so many times before. There are always a certain percentage of guys who turn out to be heels.

She said softly, slowly: 'I received a last letter from her, telling me what she was going to do. I telephoned the police at once, but when they got there it was too late.'

The shock of it was still raw to her. It was a surprise for me too. Not many dames take it that bad.

'Your sister killed herself?'

She bit her lips, closed her eyes, trying to hold back the tears.

She didn't wanna talk after that. There was a long, uncomfortable silence. A coupla courses later, she said quietly but resolutely: 'So now you know why I wanna find this man.'

'There isn't a thing you can do to him,' I pointed out. 'He hasn't committed any legal offence. Your sister didn't have to kill herself.'

'That doesn't stop me wanting to see him.'

I pushed my plate to one side, leaned my elbows on the table, thrust my face towards her. 'What kinda crazy ideas you got?'

Her brown eyes stared into mine. 'I've gotta know what kinda man he was. Don't you understand? I've gotta see him, learn what really happened between him and Pat.' Her nails were digging into the palms of her hands. 'Can't you understand what it's like to have a thing like this happen to your sister? I've just got to find him somewhere.'

'How far did you get?'

'Pat wrote me every day, told me everything about him,' she said. 'He came from Chicago. He'd spent a long time here working as an agent. But the clubs and hotels where he said he stayed when he visited Chicago don't know of him. I just can't trace him anywhere.'

'That makes it fine,' I said grimly. 'You're looking for a tall, black-bearded guy whose name probably isn't Maitland. You've got all Chicago to search and you don't even know he's here anyway.'

Her brown eyes were serious, appealing. 'That's

why I came to see you,' she said. 'I don't know anyone in Chicago. But even where I've come from, we can buy the *Chicago Chronicle*. I've read your articles, know the kinda guy you are. That's why I figured you might help me, tell me how I can trace him.'

The waiter came and took away the dessert plates. 'Coffee?' I said.

She nodded.

'Two black coffees,' I told the waiter. 'Bring two brandies with them.'

'Give me a cigarette, will you?' she asked. That was when I noticed how really strung up she was. Her fingers were trembling as she put the cigarette to her mouth.

'Finding this guy means a lot to you?'

'I've just got to know,' she whispered.

I scratched my jaw. 'It's a pretty impossible task you've set me,' I told her.

'You could write about him in your column,' she said breathlessly. 'A tall, dark man with a beard would attract plenty of attention. You'd get letters in and I could go around checking on each man we received information about.'

I said sadly: 'You've got a pretty vague idea of a reporter's job. I couldn't write up a story like that, invite folks to write in about a bearded guy. There must be a coupla thousand guys in Chicago at least who figure they look cute wearing a beard. My Editor wouldn't allow a story like that to escape further than my typewriter. He'd think I was crazy.'

Her eyes were compelling, willing me to help her. 'What do I do, then?' she asked, like she was placing her entire future life in my hands. 'What do I have to do?'

I dabbed the breadcrumbs on the tablecloth with

my forefinger, hunched my shoulders. 'Forget the idea,' I suggested.

'So you won't help me,' she said dully.

The way she said it hinted she thought I could help, but wouldn't.

'There's no way I can help.'

'If you wanted, you'd find him,' she said dully. 'If it was a good newspaper story, you'd find him. I know you'd do it.'

I hadn't the heart to be tough with her. I said evasively: 'Maybe I'll think of something.' And once again I was being a heel, remembering Janice Prescott and the way I'd promised to do something for Joe Bates too, and knowing all the time I couldn't do a thing.

Hope suddenly gleamed deep down in those brown eyes. 'You will,' she urged breathlessly. 'You'll do something to help, won't you?'

I flushed. But I'd committed myself now. 'I'll do my best,' I mumbled weakly.

Impulsively, she reached across the table, clasped my fingers, squeezed them. 'I knew you'd do something,' she said. 'I just knew you were a regular guy.'

I felt mean and uncomfortable. To cover my embarrassment, I called the waiter over and settled the bill.

'Can I drop you off somewhere?' I asked.

She sat looking at me for a long while. Then she said slowly, like she wanted to hear it all over again and be quite sure about it: 'You're going to do what you can to help, then?'

'Yeah,' I said gruffly, unable to avoid her eyes. 'I'll do what I can.'

She reached for her handbag. 'Yes, please,' she said

with sudden decision. 'Take me home.'

She told me more while I was driving. She'd drawn all her savings from the bank, come down to Chicago, taken a small furnished flat and was spending all her time trying to track Maitland. Her compelling urge to find this black-bearded guy was almost frightening in its relentlessness. It was the kinda grim determination you didn't expect a nice-looking dame to possess.

I drew into the kerb outside the tenement house where she rented her apartment. She said tonelessly: 'It's okay to leave the car here.'

She was inviting me up for a drink. Moreover she was taking it for granted it was what I expected. I didn't argue. I followed her up the drably-carpeted, dimly-lighted stairway, hovered behind her while she fumbled in her handbag for the key and opened up the door of her apartment.

The room was cheaply furnished but clean, the front door opening straight on to the lounge. A door off to the left led to the bedroom and another on the right was obviously the kitchen.

'Make yourself at home,' she said wearily. 'I'll pour you a drink.' Her actions were listless, her face kinda hard and expressionless.

I watched when she went through to the kitchen and came back with a bottle of gin and two glasses. Somehow I wasn't making contact with this dame any longer. She seemed remote, living in a world of her own. Almost, you might say, disdainful and detached from life.

She brought my drink over to me, sat on the settee alongside me, cuddling her own drink and staring into space. There was an awkward silence. I don't like awkward silences. 'All right, kid,' I said. 'How about it?'

She said dully, her voice flat and emotionless. 'Take it easy. Let me get this drink inside me, first.'

The words didn't make sense. I mentally shrugged my shoulders, abandoned proposing a toast and tried to make small conversation. 'How about you, kid?' I asked. 'How come you're not married? You're not a bad-looking dame and you've plenty on the ball.'

Her eyes flickered around to mine, stared dully, and then switched back into the world she was living in alone. 'I almost was married once,' she said in that flat voice.

'Is it rude to ask what happened?'

'He was killed.' Her voice was dead. 'There was a war.'

'I'm sorry.'

'You don't have to be,' she said. 'It happened to so many girls, and it was all so long ago.'

'Down the hatch, then,' I said, and sipped my drink.

She took a deep breath like she was steeling herself, raised the glass to her lips, threw back her head and gulped at the gin, swallowing all of it. I wasn't surprised when she began coughing and spluttering.

'That's no way to drink spirits,' I told her.

'Maybe not,' she gulped. She was having difficulty getting her breath. 'But drink gets it started quicker.'

I wanted to ask: '*Gets what started quicker?*'

'I'll pour another drink,' she said quickly, and started to climb to her feet.

I reached out, grabbed her wrists. She made no attempt to resist me, waited for me to make another move. 'You're not used to drinking, are you?'

'Obviously I'm not.' Her eyes staring into mine

were flat and emotionless.

'Then lay off it,' I advised. 'You don't have to drink to keep me company.'

'Very well,' she said hopelessly. 'If that's the way you want it.' There was a kinda cold, dull note in her voice, showing that inside she was dead and emotionless. Gently she pulled her wrists free, climbed to her feet, moved over towards the bedroom. 'I won't keep you a moment,' she said in that dead voice. She left the bedroom door half open, edged inside just beyond the range of my vision.

I stroked my jaw thoughtfully. Being a reporter is an exciting and lively occupation. But it certainly gets a guy rubbing shoulders with curious characters. Like this dame Betty. She was a good looker and class too. Understandably she was upset about her sister. But she was allowing tragedy to dominate her life, allowing it to change her into a dull, lifeless and empty shell. Almost as though she had died with her sister.

She was away maybe five minutes. I glanced up casually when she came out of the bedroom, and then the hairs on the back of my neck prickled. I watched her with my mouth going dry and my heart pounding like a steam hammer. She didn't even look towards me when she walked across to the main switch beside the door and turned off the lights.

That left only the small table lamp burning, a warm, rosy, intimate glow. Yet there was that same listlessness in her manner when, still without looking at me, she came back to the settee. She sat alongside of me and curled her legs up beneath her.

Having her that close got my heart pounding even more loudly, because that five minutes she'd spent in the bedroom had been long enough to unpin her hair and strip off almost all her clothes. All she wore now was a filmy undergarment that looked like it might tear clean away from her with one quick tug.

I gulped, pointedly tried to look away from her but found I was peeking despite myself. I cleared my throat noisily. 'You look kinda cute,' I said.

Her brown eyes were staring into space. 'Yes,' she said dully. Her voice was flat and emotionless. And that was crazy, because a dame working on me so I would make a pass at her needed more enthusiasm than that in her voice.

Not that it would necessarily have got results. Sure, she looked real cute in those under-scanties; really desirable. But a guy can quickly find himself in trouble with the nicest of dames. He can meet up with real grief with dames who don't even show him an ankle. So figure how much grief a guy can find with a dame who peels off as many layers as this one had stripped away.

'D'you need another drink?' she asked dully.

'I'm doing fine,' I said. I watched from the corner of my eye, noticed the smooth creaminess of her thighs, the generous, breathtaking swell of her milk-white breasts. She was all woman, all curves, all warm and desirable. Scanty underclothing intensified her femininity, got the palms of my hands sweating. It was like I was sweating internally, too.

'Yeah,' I panted. 'I'll do what I can to help.' I was figuring one more gulp would finish my drink, when I would climb to my feet, reach for my hat and beat it. But I'd have to beat it quick. Because this dame had more on the ball than I'd calculated from her outdoor clothes. So much on the ball I was gonna have real trouble finding the will-power to beat it while she was sitting there close to me and looking so desirable.

She said dully: 'I'm sorry I can't be more co-operative.'

I stared at her crinkling brow in perplexity. Slowly her brown eyes came around, stared into mine with a kinda hopeless resignation. 'I guess maybe it's not the way you want it,' she whispered. 'But it's the best I can do.'

I still stared. I hadn't the faintest idea what she was talking about.

She moved; moved deliberately so that a fragile shoulder-strap slipped down over her upper arm. Soft, creamy, rounded flesh seemed to engulf my vision and my senses.

'Please?' she said pleadingly.

It was difficult to breathe. Having her so close I could almost feel the heat of her, was battering down my mental defences. I tried to say: *'I'll be getting along.'* But somehow the words dried up in my throat.

Her brown eyes were tragic. 'Please,' she entreated pathetically. 'I'm not used to this. Can't you … do something? Help me … a little.'

'Sure,' I panted. 'I'll help if I can. What is it you want?'

Deep down in those brown eyes there glinted a spark of puzzlement. 'I've gone all the way as far as I can make myself,' she whispered. 'I can't go alone any further. You'll have to help now. I'm just not used to this.'

I gaped at her for long, long seconds. Then slowly I climbed to my feet, reached for my hat.

She watched me, brown eyes reflecting astonishment slowly changing to anxiety.

'You've gotta help,' she panted. 'I'm on the level with you. I just don't know about these things. I know it's not the way you'd want it, but it's the best I can do. You've got to understand. I'm ready, but ... I just don't feel anything inside me.'

I looked at her levelly. I said quietly: 'Will you tell me just one thing?'

Her eyes widened.

'What the hell are you driving at?' I demanded. 'Just how am I supposed to help?'

Her eyes were wide, staring like she couldn't believe her ears. She panted anxiously. 'You're going to help me, aren't you? You're going to trace John Maitland.'

'If I can,' I said guardedly. 'If I can.'

A tiny frown puckered her forehead. 'But if you help me, if you give up your time, don't you expect ...' She broke off, and suddenly I knew what was in her mind. In a way it was almost insulting.

I said grimly, laying it on the line so we could both know what we were talking about: 'You're figuring on payment in kind?'

She flushed at my bluntness. 'Isn't that the way you want it?'

'What gives you that idea?' I snarled.

She dropped her eyes. 'That's the way you expect it. That's the way men think, isn't it?'

I glared at her, swallowing my anger. It was difficult to believe she really believed what she was saying. Somewhere along the line someone had given me a real dirty character.

'Listen, kid,' I said grimly. 'I'll help you if I can, but you're way off beam. If I can help folks, I don't do it for payment.' I took a deep breath. 'And when a nice kid like you, a straight kid ...' I broke off, gulped, started again. 'The last thing I want ...' I broke off once more, stared at her, felt the palms of my hands sweating and the blood hissing through my veins. 'For Pete's sake,' I panted. 'Put something on, willya. What d'ya think I am, a stone image?'

She stared at me like she didn't dare believe her ears. Then swiftly she slipped off the settee and ran through to the bedroom.

She got back maybe a minute later wearing a silk dressing-gown drawn in at the waist. My pulse had slowed and my blood pressure eased down a coupla points. 'You crazy kid,' I growled. 'Where d'you get that crazy idea?'

She smiled wryly. She had plaintive, little-girl eyes. She said simply: 'I've read your books.'

'Read them again,' I snarled. 'Either you don't read good, or I don't write good.'

'You really will help me just the same?' Her voice was pleading, but her eyes shining. Warmth was flowing back into her like she was coming alive again. She musta been under the strain of forcing herself all through dinner.

'Yeah,' I grunted. 'I'll help if I can.' I took a coupla strides towards the door, stopped with my hand on the door handle. 'I'm promising nothing,' I warned.

She came right up close, and now her eyes showed she was not only alive but grateful and ... yeah, I've gotta say it, almost adoring!

'You're a good guy,' she said softly. 'I knew you'd help me. I could tell you were kind from the way you wrote. Sure, you're a good guy.'

'Chances are I won't be able to do a thing.'

'You will,' she said, with a confidence that surprised me. 'You will.' She kept looking at me tenderly, kept looking so long that it suddenly happened quite naturally, both of us moving at the same time so her arms were around my neck as my hands encircled her waist.

Her cheek was against mine, and the scent of her was sweet and tantalising. 'You're a good guy,' she whispered, and there was a choke in her voice. 'You're a real good guy.'

I could feel the heat of her body burning through the silk, and the firmness of her hips. I was remembering her sitting there, a fragile, slipping shoulder-strap and the flowering towards me. I said hoarsely: 'You've gotta let me go, kid. I've gotta go. D'ya understand? I've gotta get outta here. You're a good kid. So help me help you stay that way?'

'You're a nice guy,' she whispered, and her breath was hot and moist against my ear.

Her soft skin was moving beneath the silk, a subtle, tantalising tingle running up from my fingers to my brain. And all the time, I could see the fragile strap slipping lower and lower, firmly rounded flesh blossoming towards me. 'Be smart, will you?' I gritted. 'Let me go, damn you?'

She let me go; slowly and reluctantly.

I opened the door quickly, pushed outside quickly. My forehead was damp and the palms of my hands burning. The expression in her eyes now showed me I wouldn't have to help her at all. Right now everything had changed.

'I'll be in touch with you, honey,' I panted.

She was breathing hard. 'You're a good guy,' she whispered. 'A real good guy.'

'Say goodbye and help me stay good.'

'Even if I don't say goodbye, you'll still be a good guy.'

It was touch and go. The door was still open and she was still standing there, hot and desirable. I was balanced on the razor-edge of being a good guy or a bad guy. And right then she wouldn't have cared how bad I was.

But I cared. I had to right any wrong impressions she may have got about me.

'I'll be around, kid,' I said. 'I'll be seeing you.'

It needed all my self-control to turn on my heel, stride along the corridor and clatter down the stairs. I could sense her standing in the doorway watching me, her eyes drilling into the back of my neck.

I crossed the pavement, climbed down behind the steering wheel of my car.

My hands were still sweating.

'*Listen, fella,*' I told myself. '*You promised to help the dame. That's what you're gonna do. You've gotta help the dame. Maybe afterwards, maybe afterwards.*'

I turned the key in the ignition and stamped on the gas. I knew I was gonna be a long while getting off to sleep that night.

7

For the next coupla days I had trouble with the phone. Janice Prescott rang me maybe a dozen times. Each time, I answered in a gruff voice, said Mr Janson was out on an assignment. There was just nothing I could do to help Joe Bates. But I hadn't the guts to tell her outright there was nothing anyone could do. In any case, in just a few days Joe Bates would be out of jail and not needing help.

Betty Scott also rang, and that was different. I'd have spoken to her, but I really was out on an assignment when she came through. She left a message. A brief message, but one that hit hard. *'I rely on you!'*

Then Billy called around at the office and threw a scare into me. I didn't want the *Chronicle*'s reputation subjected to even the slightest criticism.

I telephoned frantic instructions for Billy to be kept in the waiting room while messengers were hastily sent to round up two of the observers from the theatre. One guy was a bank teller and the other a drug store assistant. I spoke to their employers, who gave them time off, and Billy wasn't allowed upstairs until both observers were flanking him like sentinels and had assured themselves, by questioning the downstairs staff, that Billy hadn't even had a smell of the Chief's office where the sealed envelope was on show.

Billy said courteously, politely and with the right amount of reserve, like him and me hadn't ever been properly introduced: 'I should very much like the privilege of talking to your Editor for a few minutes.' He paused momentarily, and a smile touched his lips. 'In the presence of witnesses of course.'

The Chief's always busy. But he wasn't so busy he couldn't spare time to foster a good news story. Every day now, the *Chicago Chronicle* was running an item in a black-edged box titled 'Los Guitanos'. We had to keep Los Guitanos alive until Saturday when the envelope was opened. An interview between the Editor and Billy would be a life-giving injection to the story.

There were maybe a dozen of us filed into the Chief's office; the two observers from the theatre, myself and Billy and a half-dozen other guys who'd been pulled in off the streets as witnesses. A coupla *Chronicle* photographers burned flash bulbs, angling the Chief smiling across his desk at Billy with the witnesses in the background and the sealed envelope hanging on the wall behind the Chief's head.

After the acrid smell of the flashlights had drifted away and we'd finished coughing and blinking our eyes, the Chief settled back in his chair, looped his thumbs in his pants' suspenders and rolled his cigar from one corner of his mouth to the other. 'Now what can I do for you?' he asked, and his blue eyes were resting gently on Billy with childlike interest.

Billy sat up straight, squared his shoulders, glanced around to make sure everyone was listening intently, and then said, with an air of confidence that made me weak at the knees: 'When the opened envelope reveals Los Guitanos have correctly forecast your next Saturday headlines, I assume your photographers and reporters will be present.'

'Naturally,' said the Chief. His voice was wondering, like he was trying to figure the catch.

Billy said seriously: 'I am anxious that all precautions shall be taken to satisfy everyone there has been no possibility of trickery.'

'Naturally we shall do our best to ensure that,' said the Chief drily.

Billy took a deep breath. 'Would you have any objections,' he asked, 'if reporters and photographers from other newspapers are also present on Saturday when the envelope is opened?'

The Chief did have objections. It was a *Chronicle* scoop and he wanted the exclusive story. But Billy's request was reasonable and could only be refused with reflection upon the *Chronicle*. The Chief was quick to see the possibilities, too. Other newspapers would have to give publicity to the *Chronicle*.

'I don't see any objections,' drawled the Chief.

Billy smiled with satisfaction. His smile seemed to embrace everyone. My knees were still rubbery. Knowing what I did, and knowing that on Saturday he'd be shaking the dust of Chicago from his feet, I wondered at his colossal nerve, even envied him for it.

Billy said tentatively: 'I hope you appreciate my difficulties, Mr Healey. This is the first time I've performed in Chicago and I am at a disadvantage. I am not personally acquainted with the editors of Chicago's newspapers. If you would be good enough to give me letters of introduction, I am sure it would result in their full co-operation.'

I was sure of it too. The editors of our rival papers

would be falling over themselves to share in the public interest we were whipping up.

The Chief sighed: 'Certainly I'll do that,' he said regretfully.

'I'm very grateful,' said Billy sincerely.

I didn't get it.

I didn't get it one little bit. Billy had admitted he hadn't an earthly of pulling this off. The smart thing was for him to soft-pedal and slip out of town quietly. This way, he was rubbing the noses of everyone in Chicago into the miserable failure of his Casino boast.

Yet maybe he was still hoping I'd fix it for him, although I'd been honest and told him I couldn't and wouldn't rig it. Now, with other newspapers taking an interest and watching the *Chronicle*, Billy was killing any slender hope he may have had that I'd help.

I wanted to exchange a few words with Billy but, with all those folks watching, I daren't. I wasn't kidding myself either. It wasn't Billy who really interested me. It was Lucy who'd captured my interest, Lucy with her warm, vital body; Lucy the pocket-Venus with her girlish curves unconcealed by scanty trappings, two black strands of silk and a pen-wiper.

Followed by witnesses, I escorted Billy to the exit doors of the *Chronicle*, watched him airily wave for a taxi and smilingly pose for the photographers, flourishing the letters of introduction the Chief had written.

Then moodily I returned to my office. Meeting Billy had made me think of Lucy. Thinking of Lucy made me think of those things nature intended guys to think about. That got me thinking of Betty Scott and the determined way she's stalked me, made me promise to help her, and thinking about her fragile, slipping shoulder-strap.

I wanted to do as she'd asked and help find this guy Maitland, who'd given her sister so much mental torment. But finding a tall, black-bearded guy – whose real name probably wasn't Maitland anyway – somewhere among the two hundred million inhabitants of the United States, was a tall order.

I'd got a coupla detective agents, who owed me favours, working on it. Friendly cops at police headquarters were running through their files for me when they got a slack moment. But I wasn't hopeful.

Therefore even if Betty Scott did speak to me on the telephone, that was as far as it would go.

Because I didn't intend to be too much of a heel. If I met Betty Scott again, I had a pretty good idea what was gonna happen. She had too. It was what she wanted and it was what I wanted.

But that streak of obstinacy I've got inside me wouldn't square itself with my conscience. I wanted to show Betty I was worthy of the confidence she'd placed in me first. My attitude may have been stupid. But it was human.

I didn't wanna meet Betty Scott again unless I could justify her confidence and give her useful information about Maitland.

And deep down inside me, I knew there wasn't a chance in hell I'd ever locate him.

8

When we put the last edition to bed on Friday night I was still thinking about Lucy. Still thinking about Betty too. And the more time that passed without me seeing them made the memory of them grow more vivid in my imagination.

I went to bed that Friday night still thinking about them and unable to sleep because of them. I tossed and turned in the darkness, thinking of them and trying not to, until sleep finally caught up with me.

Sleep should have ended my problems. It didn't. Because it made them more real, made everything so much tougher!

Because sleeping, I had both of them. Lucy was one side of me, vital, alive and burning, looking at me tenderly while her youthful curves strained to escape from the black silken strands. Betty was the other side, her brown eyes sincere and longing, that fragile shoulder-strap slipping, slipping, seeming never to stop slipping and revealing.

'You've gotta help me, Hank,' whispered Betty, and she kinda flowed towards me, flowed over me, so that the softness of her and the sweet smell of her engulfed me.

'I can read your mind,' said Lucy, her voice loaded with husky entreaty. She was hovering above me, lips hot and moist and the weight of her firm curves overflowing the black strands of silk.

Desire welled up inside me so strong I almost choked. I moved my arms to gather them up and strain them against me, taste and savour the hot, sweet warmness of them. I felt the sweat rolling down my face, when my arms wouldn't move and hung limply at my sides like I had no power over them.

I tried to move my legs, to move my body, to raise my shoulders from the bed. Sweat drenched me, poured from me with the strain of my wild efforts. And all the time, they hovered over me, came lower and closer, their exciting nearness driving me crazy as I strained to force my brain to control my body. But my brain was detached from my body, unable to motivate it, unable to force it to respond, and all the time their moist, wet, warm lips brushed my cheeks and touched my lips, and the softness of their skins sent fiery shafts of desire burning through my body.

I exerted all my remaining strength to move my leaden limbs, poured with sweat as the mounting desire inside me was harshly frustrated.

Then the monotonous, discordant jangle of the telephone, resounding compellingly.

I sat up in bed and switched on the bedside light. The dream was so real, it was difficult to believe I was alone. So real, my pyjamas were soaked with sweat like I'd come in from the sea.

The telephone jangled at me.

I reached out a moist hand, lifted the receiver. 'What the hell ...?' I growled.

Detective Inspector Blunt's calm, clear voice came down the line, hard and cutting. 'Get sleep out of your eyes, Janson.,' he rapped. 'I've been ringing two minutes solid.'

The memory of them was slipping into the background of my mind. My sweat-soaked pyjamas were uncomfortably cold in the night air. 'What the hell?' I snarled. 'I was sleeping. A guy's entitled to sleep some time.'

'You want I should let you go back to sleep?' he asked grimly.

It suddenly hit me then. Blunt telephoning in the middle of the night! He wasn't the kinda guy who played tricks. I thrust both dames right out of my mind, blinked myself into wakefulness. 'It's something important?' I guessed.

'You wouldn't wanna miss this, Janson.'

'I'm listening.'

'Preston Williams's wife,' he said curtly. 'She's been found. I'm going over there right away. Gotta pass your apartment. Be ready in five minutes and I'll pick you up.'

'You're going to her!'

'Yeah,' he said grimly. 'She's dead.'

I sat with the dead receiver in my hand for maybe thirty seconds before I digested the information. Then I slapped down the receiver, climbed out of bed and made a dive for the bathroom. I stripped off my pyjamas, towelled myself dry and climbed into my clothes like I got a hundred bucks for every second saved doing it.

Even then, I was only just in time. The headlights of the squad car swung around the block and sped towards me as I walked down the steps of my apartment.

The car snarled into the kerb, slowed, and I'd ripped open the door and climbed inside with Blunt before it stopped. The driver fed gas to the engine and, as the surge of speed pressed me back against the cushions, Blunt grunted:

'Lucky for you; I wouldn't have waited.'

'You've found her?' I panted. 'How dead?'

'Very dead,' he said humourlessly.

I knew by his attitude he didn't wanna speak. He was a cautious guy. He preferred to let facts speak for themselves.

We sat in silence for maybe five minutes while the car tore on through the night. Then I asked: 'Where we heading?'

'About twenty miles outta town,' he said. 'Road repair gang found them.'

'Them?' I echoed.

His clear grey eyes stared at me levelly. 'Let's wait and see for ourselves, shall we?' he asked softly. 'Right now I don't know any more than you. Let's wait, huh?'

'Okay,' I said wearily. 'Okay. I'll wait.' I dug my hands deep into my mackintosh pockets, pressed myself back against the cushions, closed my eyes and tried to coax myself back into my dream.

Only this time, it was gonna be different. This time, my mind was gonna have full control of my body and motivate it. I was doing nicely at that, melting back into my dream and half-way to the point where Blunt had interrupted.

Then the car driver slammed on the brakes, and Blunt's elbow was gouging my ribs. 'Are you coming, or do you wanna finish dreaming?'

I blinked myself into wakefulness, shot a swift, suspicious glance at Blunt, for one dreadful moment scared he'd known what I'd been dreaming. But his broad shoulders were looming against the night sky in the doorway as he climbed out of the car.

I followed him sheepishly.

There were six cops already drawn into the side of the road, and uniformed cops milling around.

A cop with a powerful flashlamp led the way through a gap freshly broken in the hedge, down through the undergrowth into a gully and along into a copse, which was maybe a hundred yards away from the road.

A battery of arc lights had been rigged up so they bathed the scene in a fierce white light.

Grimly Blunt led the way, with me following at his heels. We stood side by side, staring down at what lay in the centre of the spotlight glare.

I've seen some unpleasant things in my time. I've seen dead guys and I've seen live guys hurt so bad they oughtta have been dead. I've seen more stiffs under white sheets in the morgue than most guys have relatives, and I've grown a stomach that should be cast-iron. But I felt sick. Good and sick.

Blunt's voice was shaky too. He asked one of the plainclothes dicks standing nearby: 'Has anything been touched?'

'Nothing, sir. Everything's ready, waiting for you to give the okay.'

Blunt said quietly: 'All right. Go ahead.'

He stepped to one side so the dicks with their flashlights and measuring sticks could start meticulously recording everything.

I went with him. I tipped my fedora to the back of my head with my forefinger, dug down for my breast-pocket handkerchief and mopped my forehead. Getting out of bed in the middle of the night doesn't put a guy on top of the world. But it doesn't make him feel bad the way I felt then, either.

And I felt real bad!

The divisional surgeon drifted over, fat, chubby and smiling gently. He rested his black doctor's bag on the ground, thrust his hands into his trouser pockets, rocked back on his heels, and stared at us both with a glint of amusement in his eyes.

'What's so funny?' snarled Blunt.

'You both look kinda green.'

'I never before saw two folks with their faces blown away,' gritted Blunt.

The surgeon smiled gently. 'Three weeks is a long time,' he said. 'There's been rain, there's been sun and there's insects too. You ever seen what happens to a piece of meat left out in a field for three weeks?'

Blunt said nothing.

I said nothing.

'That's the way fishermen get worms for bait,' the surgeon said calmly. He was watching us closely like it gave him a kick to see us uncomfortable. 'Won't be so bad where their clothes have protected them,' he admitted generously, like it was a comforting thought.

Blunt took my arm. 'Let's get back to the car. No point in waiting here.'

We walked back to the car in silence, sat side by side on the back seat. I pulled out a cigarette, offered one to Blunt. When we were both alight, I asked: 'How d'you know it's Mrs Williams?'

He exhaled smoke slowly. He said in a hard, grim voice: 'The first of my men to arrive after the discovery saw a handbag lying beside them. He opened it up. Mrs Williams's security card was inside.'

'Then who is the guy with her?'

He sighed. 'What time does the morning edition go to press?'

'Late as possible,' I told him. 'First copy hits the streets at five o'clock.'

He glanced at his wrist-watch. 'Just half past two,' he commented drily. 'So let's be patient, huh? Let the facts sort themselves out. Just sit tight, will ya?'

Twenty minutes dragged by, and then three dicks came over, waited while me and Blunt climbed out from the car.

'All finished?' asked Blunt.

'The bodies are being taken to the mortuary right now,' said one dick. 'We've taken photographs, measured up all around, and searched them.' Another dick held up a brown briefcase. 'Everything's in here,' he said.

'No footprints,' went on the first dick. 'Been a bit of rain and everything's been washed clean.'

'Anything else?' asked Blunt grimly.

The third dick spoke then. He was a ballistics specialist. He said in a dull, monotonous voice: 'Not much doubt what happened. They sat or lay down close together with a coupla Mills bomb hanging around their necks. Every indication of a joint suicide pact. Both bomb pins drawn simultaneously. They were still holding the bomb pins in their hands.'

'Why d'you say suicide?' asked Blunt.

The dick with the briefcase patted it meaningfully. 'Suicide letter,' he said. 'Addressed to the coroner. The fella had the letter in his hip pocket with a batch of other stuff. Fella name of Maitland, John Maitland.'

John Maitland!

For a moment everything around me became

swimmy and wavery. *John Maitland! That guy.* Like digging in the desert to find a needle and finding it! Like a starving man having a great wad of dollars flung at him so hard it hurt.

John Maitland!

The world stopped swaying, steadied to normality. The clear voice of Blunt was talking, and vaguely I heard the replies the dicks gave.

John Maitland.

Blunt said: 'Unusual way of killing yourself. First time I've hit up against suicides using bombs.'

'It makes sure,' said one dick.

'Listen, Blunt,' I panted. 'Let me have a look at those documents, will ya? Let me have a look at that suicide letter, will ya?'

I was over-excited. I sensed all four of them looking at me strangely. I drew out my pocket handkerchief, wiped the palms of my hands. 'I wanna make sure I spell the name right,' I explained weakly.

'Yeah, I can imagine,' said Blunt bleakly. He jerked his head. 'Let's get back to the headquarters. We can go through the stuff in comfort.'

Back in Blunt's office, beneath the strong glare of the desk light, we went through everything. There wasn't any doubt it was Mrs Preston Williams's handbag. In addition to the usual clutter a woman carries around in her handbag, we found her driving licence, her social security card, visiting cards and a cheque book.

There wasn't any doubt about it being John Maitland either. In addition to the suicide letter stating he and Mrs Williams couldn't bear to go on living apart any longer, there were three letters in his breast pocket that would have made Mrs Williams think twice about that Mills bomb if she had read them.

Those three letters were from dames. Each letter competed with the others in its tenderness, sincerity and protestations of love and devotion. Two of the letters came from dames I'd never heard of. The third came from Clinton and was the more recently dated. I gulped, felt my mouth go dry, as I saw the signature, *Pat Scott*, at the foot of the letter.

Betty's sister!

'What's biting you?' asked Blunt, staring at me curiously.

'Nothing,' I said weakly. 'Just short of sleep, I guess.' I was all twisted up inside.

Blunt leafed through John Maitland's diary. Written in Maitland's writing, the same as that of the letter to the coroner, was his Chicago address.

Blunt gave crisp, clear-cut orders. 'We have to get identification. Send along to Maitland's address, get somebody to identify him. Better write off to these three girls too. Just in case we need them for identification.'

I could have told him Pat Scott wouldn't be replying, but I remembered Betty's soulful brown eyes, and kept my lip buttoned.

'Send someone else to the cemetery,' instructed Blunt. 'Superintendent Williams must have the news broken to him.' For a moment, Blunt's steely grey eyes flicked to mine. 'Looks like I was on the wrong scent, Hank,' he admitted. 'Williams didn't kill his wife for her dough after all.'

'Guess not,' I grunted.

'I want all reports by the morning,' went on Blunt. 'Ballistics will confirm the type and method of use of the bombs. Post mortem and pathologist's reports required.'

He glanced up at me. 'Anything more you want, Hank?'

I passed my hand over my forehead. 'I can't think of anything.'

'What's eating you?' he demanded. 'It's getting good and late if you want to get it in the morning edition.'

Imagine that! I was so knocked off balance by John Maitland dropping right into my lap, I'd completely forgotten I was on a hot story.

I caught a taxi over to the office, telephoned the Chief, who was at home in bed, and settled down behind my typewriter.

It was a grim story. I didn't have to dress it up to make it sound gruesome. I just had to write it up the way I saw it. It wasn't a job I liked doing. My memory was too vivid.

By the time I was through writing, the Chief had arrived at the office and was ripping out the front page make-up he'd prepared earlier and rearranging it so my story would top everything.

I carried my typed story through to his office, placed it on the desk in front of him.

'Better look through it,' I said wearily. 'You're gonna agree this justifies getting you out of bed.'

He took a long while reading through it. Finally he nodded his head in approval. 'Yeah,' he agreed gruffly. 'I like my bed as much as the next guy. But this is hot. I ain't never heard of folks killing themselves with Mills bombs before.'

He half-handed me my copy, withdrew it like he had second thoughts, and reached for his blue pencil. I watched him listlessly. He poised his blue pencil, then with a firm, vigorous stroke crossed out my banner headline.

SUICIDES USE BOMBS.

I watched him carefully pencil in a different headline.

SUICIDES BOMB PACT

'You didn't like my headline, huh?' I asked.

His blue eyes stared up levelly into mine. There was the faintest suggestion of a twinkle in them when he said: 'I guess my headline is no better than yours. I just wanted to make it more difficult for Los Guitanos.'

That was when I got it. I hadn't given Billy another thought until now. But this was the headline Lucy was supposed to have foreseen. This was the headline supposed to be written out in the sealed envelope now resting in the office safe.

And if I'd had a million dollars, I'd have bet every cent that no-one could have looked into the future and prophesied *that* headline.

9

I wanted to rush straight round to Betty Scott and prove her faith in me had been justified, and that I'd found – John Maitland. It was gonna be easy to get credit for tracking him. Too easy. But I'd been helping like she asked, hadn't I?

But it was five o'clock in the morning when I left the *Chronicle* offices. The early morning edition bundles with the ink still wet were hurtling down the delivery chutes to the waiting news vans.

Five o'clock in the morning is no time to be thumbing the doorbell of a dame's apartment, no matter how urgent. And this wasn't urgent. John Maitland wasn't going anywhere. Not any more … ever!

I needed sleep, too. I needed rest so bad, I was asleep the moment my head touched the pillow. When next my eyes opened at eleven o'clock in the morning, I was so late I hadn't even time to think about Betty Scott.

I had exactly one hour to get washed, dressed and be ready at the *Chronicle* offices in time for the dramatic opening of the envelope containing the prediction of Los Guitanos.

I cu myself while shaving, dressed hurriedly while

coffee was brewing, and gulped it down so hastily I scalded my mouth. And all the time, I was telling myself what a fool waste of time it was. Because by now Billy and Lucy were comfortably settled in a train headed West, putting as many miles as possible between themselves and Chicago before the storm broke.

Yeah, they wouldn't be able to face up to the storm of ridicule the press of Chicago would bring down around their ears when that envelope was opened and somebody read out what Lucy had written.

What the hell had she written anyway?

But even without Billy, I had to be there on time. I was the guy who had handled this deal from the start. I just had to be there!

I crashed three red lights getting to the office, parked my car around back and panted into the newsroom just as four observers from the Casino theatre ceremoniously drew the sealed envelope from the safe.

There were so many reporters and photographers from other newspapers, there wasn't room for us all in the Chief's office. We overflowed back into the newsroom.

And then I saw Billy!

He was smiling with self-assurance and confidence, surrounded by reporters and talking with machine-gun rapidity while their pencils flew over the paper.

His cool, bare-faced cheek made me feel weak. He was being crazy. I've known guys who had bold-faced effrontery. But right then, looking at Billy as he beamed around with satisfaction, I knew I was watching someone who had more cool, more cold-blooded nerve than I ever hoped to possess.

Just figure it. All those reporters and

photographers burning to laugh and ridicule him out of his profession. And he was revelling in it. Enjoying it.

The four observers hadn't once taken their eyes off the sealed envelope. Carefully they propped it on the Chief's desk for the photographers, who manoeuvred Healey and Billy into position, flashed shots of them.

My mouth was dry and my throat muscles tight and choking. I glanced up at the clock on the wall, and it was five minutes to twelve. Either Billy was gonna take a real panning, or within the next five minutes he was gonna try and pull something really smart. I watched him like a hawk.

I wasn't the only one. Everybody was watching him intently. And because he knew it, Billy kept well away from the envelope, didn't go within five yards of it.

'Hey, Janson,' called a reporter. 'Whad'ya got to say about all this? Is your test gonna floor Los Guitanos, or do you believe in clairvoyance?'

Everyone was watching, listening for my reply. Everyone, that is, except Billy. He was tapping a reporter on the shoulder, trying to attract his attention.

I cleared my throat. I said hoarsely: 'At five o'clock this morning, nobody knew the headlines of today's *Chronicle*. Note even those who wrote them. The headlines refer to a bomb suicide.' I took a deep breath. 'That envelope, and whatever is written on the paper it contains, has been in this office for most part of this week. Last night it was locked in the office safe. Four observers, members of the audience from the Casino, are the only ones to have touched that envelope since last night, and they removed it from the safe in full view of everyone.'

I took another deep breath. 'That envelope has been in the safe since six o'clock last night until just a few minutes ago. The bodies of the suicides were discovered at two o'clock this morning. If therefore the headlines of today's *Chronicle* are correctly forecast and written on the paper inside the envelope, I shall be compelled to acknowledge the existence of clairvoyance and the ability of Los Guitanos to see into the future.'

There were a few handclaps, a few chuckles, a few sneers, and a lanky photographer grabbed me by the shoulder, manoeuvred me around so he could get a photograph of me with the sealed envelope in the background.

Four or five other photographers were angling their cameras. I stood there feeling sheepish.

'Don't worry, Hank,' grinned a photographer. 'This is quite painless.' He went around back of me, altered my pose, wiped the shine off the glass enclosing the envelope and went back to his camera.

On the other side of the room, Billy was talking self-importantly, carefully watched by everyone.

I blinked as the flashbulbs burned out one after the other in quick succession.

'That's fine,' the photographer told me. 'Now let's have one of you holding the envelope.'

I picked up the envelope, held it high. He came around back of me, adjusted my position again. 'Use the other hand,' he said. He took the envelope, placed it in my other hand.

I stood there feeling silly while the photographers angled and took more shots.

The Chief cleared his throat, said in a loud, commanding voice: 'Attention everybody. Listen, everybody, please.'

There was a sudden hush. Everyone looked at the clock. There was thirty seconds to go before twelve o'clock.

'Will the observers please take the envelope?' said the Chief.

The observers stepped forward, took the envelope from me.

'Have you anything to say before the envelope is opened?' the Chief asked Billy.

'Yes,' said Billy, stepping forward confidently, basking in the attention he was getting. 'I want to say this. I hope that after my partner's prediction is proved to be correct, a representative of the *Chicago Chronicle* will attend at the Casino tonight to make an announcement.'

Billy musta been outta his mind bluffing it this far. Yet he spoke with such conviction he almost had me convinced too.

Maybe he had even had Healey convinced. The Chief said without hesitation: 'The *Chronicle* will be pleased to make such a public announcement.'

'Very well, then,' said Billy, calmly and confidently. 'I am ready.'

Billy didn't wait to be asked. He walked right over to the far side of the room, at least a dozen yards from the observers who were holding the envelope.

'All right,' said the Chief. 'Open up.'

I guess to those observers all this seemed a loada dramatic poppy-cock. I imagine there wasn't one person in that room who thought there was one chance in hell Lucy coulda guessed that day's headlines. But the observers were ordinary working men, revelling in a change from the monotony of their routine life. They went about opening that envelope with all due seriousness like it was a religious ritual.

One of them held the envelope while another very

carefully snipped the sealed tape tied around it. Two other observers watched intently like students in an operating theatre.

The tapes dropped to the floor, the two thin sheets of glass separated, and the envelope was removed from between them. The third observer took the envelope, and with great solemnity thrust his finger beneath the flap and eased it open.

The fourth observer, with his finger and thumb extended like he was picking up a cockroach, dug down into the envelope, drew out the slip of paper.

I was watching his face intently. So we all were, except for an occasional sharp glance we darted at Billy. There was still that smile of confidence on his face as he stood patiently at the far side of the room.

The observer very slowly and deliberately opened up the folded sheet. He had an expressive face. A kinda elastic face that reflected every fleeting emotion, mirrored everything he was thinking.

And what he was thinking was that he was gonna get a lot of useful publicity outta this, that he'd be the guy who knew before everyone else what was written on that slip, and that he hadn't the faintest doubt the conditions of the test would expose Los Guitanos to ridicule. He was even getting ready to gloat over them.

The paper crackled in his fingers. He opened it upside down so he had to turn it around to read it. His eyes were smiling sadistically as they began to read.

Then it was like all his thought processes had been paralysed. He stared. He went on staring. Slowly his jaw sagged and the gloating expression melted from his eyes to be replaced by astonishment. Astounded astonishment.

In that crowded room it was so silent I could hear

the ticking of that clock!

We watched the observer breathlessly. The observer stared at the paper. Then slowly the observer's eyes came up, stared around at us. His mouth gaped open.

'Well, read it, man,' snapped Healey. 'That's what you're here for. Read it.'

The observer swallowed, tried to say something, couldn't get the words out.

One of the other observers snatched the paper, glanced at it, read aloud:

Suicides Bomb Pact.

There was a kinda hushed silence. The man who had read it aloud suddenly stopped looking efficient, peered back again at the paper in his hands like he couldn't believe his eyes. He read again in a hoarse voice: 'Suicides Bomb Pact!' This time he said it like he couldn't believe it.

I couldn't believe it either. I took four swift paces, glanced over his shoulder. The words were pencilled there firmly and clearly. Yet still I couldn't believe it.

Suicides Bomb Pact!

It was incredible. It was unbelievable. It couldn't be happening. Nobody, not even a sweet dame like Lucy, could see into the future this way, prophecy days in advance the headlines springing from an event that hadn't then happened.

Everyone was crowding around now, staring at the clearly-printed words on the paper, trying hard to believe that this was really happening. And above the gasps of surprise and disbelief, I could hear Billy's rich baritone, reciting for the benefit of the reporters. 'This is conclusive proof of the mystic powers of my partner. This is the complete answer to all the sceptics; the only clairvoyance act willing to submit to such a test.'

There was movement now, excitement and wonder, surging through everyone. The reporters were gathering around Billy, photographing him for the hundredth time, catching his words like they were falling pearls.

I felt weak and shaky. I made my way to a corner of the room, leaned against the wall. The Chief came alongside me. His blue eyes were wide and mystified. 'How the hell does he work that?'

'It's incredible,' I panted. 'I can't believe it.'

'D'you think the guy's really genuine?' asked the Chief, doubtfully.

I remembered Billy's distress, the way he'd admitted he'd have to leave town. But surely this was conclusive proof? Since that message had been written and placed in the envelope, he hadn't been within yards of it. Maybe he'd been fooling me that night. Lucy really *was* different. Maybe she *did* have exceptional powers. Maybe she *could* see into the future!

I said weakly: 'It beats me. It just don't seem possible.'

His thoughts were paralleling mine. 'Figure it all the way along the line, Hank,' he reasoned. 'Is there a weak link anywhere? Could he have got at that envelope? Is there any way he could have got at it?'

I shook my head. 'Not one,' I said. 'From the time it was written until now, he hasn't once touched it. Neither has his partner.'

'Can such things be?' breathed the Chief.

'You mean, can people see into the future?'

'Looks like this dame's done it.'

Billy was surrounded by reporters. They were ushering him towards the door. He kinda searched around, found me, called to me loudly in his rich voice: 'Mr Janson!'

I straightened up. 'Yeah?' I said weakly.

'You'll be at the Casino tonight to make the announcement?'

I looked at the Chief. He nodded.

'I'll be there.' I said.

'Thank you, Mr Janson,' said Billy, and then he allowed himself to be swept outside by the clamouring reporters.

'Tell you what you do now, Hank,' said the Chief. 'I got a phone call just before this started. That guy Maitland's going to be identified. Detective Inspector Blunt thought you'd like to be along.'

'Fine,' I said weakly. 'That's just what I need now. A nice long gander at a stiff, white and faceless corpse. That'll brace me up no end.'

'And don't forget the Casino tonight,' he added as I reached for my fedora.

10

When I arrived at Blunt's office, he had with him a tall, lean guy with hair so fair it was almost white. He was a young guy, about my own age, slender but athletic, good-looking except maybe for his crew-cut hair style that makes a guy look like he's just come out of stir.

'This is William Jackson,' Blunt said in introduction.

I nodded at him.

He nodded back.

'John Maitland was lodging with him,' explained Blunt.

I looked at Jackson with renewed interest. 'You knew the guy,' I said. 'You were a friend of his.'

Jackson smiled wryly. 'Friend of his hardly,' he said wryly. 'I barely knew him. A few months ago, I advertised for a young man to share my apartment. Maitland came along. He was a nice enough guy, paid three months in advance, and kept to himself. He was a secretive kinda guy, never talked about himself. During the whole time he was with me, I hardly ever saw him. He used to go out at nights when I was in, and come home after I'd gone off to work in the morning.'

'What kinda guy was he?' I persisted.

He shrugged his shoulders, and his long, muscular frame seemed ill at ease in the armchair he occupied. 'A tall fella,' he said. 'About my height. Long black hair and a black beard. Don't know what his job was. He travelled around a great deal.'

'Did you know anything about his interests?' I persisted. 'About Mrs Williams, I mean. Did you have any idea he was friendly with her …?'

'I'm sorry, fella,' he interrupted gently. 'I guess really I hardly knew the guy. He shared my apartment, had a room of his own. In all those months, I never saw him more than a coupla dozen times, exchanged only a word or two with him. He was that kinda guy.'

Blunt said dryly: 'Mr Jackson has been very helpful. I suspect he is too truthful to fabricate stories that might prove sensational enough for your newspaper. I think all we can reasonably expect from Mr Jackson is identification of Maitland.'

'Can you do that?' I shot at Jackson. 'He's kinda mussed up.'

'I guess so,' he said slowly. 'You see, there's one thing I noticed about him. The moles on his left arm. A coupla times I've seen him with his shirt sleeves rolled up. That's one of the things I've noticed.'

'I've warned you already, Jackson,' said Blunt quietly. 'This isn't gonna be a pleasant sight.'

'I didn't think it would be,' said Jackson quietly. 'Mills bombs can be quite messy.'

Blunt led the way, Jackson followed and I strung along in the rear. There was really no need for me to be there, but Blunt was playing ball, keeping me in touch with every development. I had to play ball too.

It was cold down there in the morgue. They were

the only two there, bulking stiffly beneath the white sheets as they lay still and cold.

'This is the one,' said Blunt, and stripped the covering from the longer of the two sheeted mounds.

Maitland had been cleaned up considerably, the messy, bloodied parts washed away and his clothes stripped off. But it still made me feel queer looking at that faceless corpse.

It gave Jackson a tough time, too. He clenched his hands tightly together and bit his lip. But he was determined to stand up to his ordeal. He deliberately stared down at Maitland's body, stared at the faceless, empty, broken brain pan, the tufts of black hair that still remained, and slowly ran his eye down to the left arm, which lay rigid and stiff like wax.

'Those are his moles,' said Jackson. His voice was cracked and strained.

'That's lucky,' breathed Blunt. 'Decomposition nearly reached up to there.'

'It's him right enough,' said Jackson hoarsely. 'There's not the slightest doubt of that.'

Blunt said: 'You mentioned he wore a black beard?'

'That's right,' said Jackson. 'The first time I saw him he wore a black beard. But he shaved it off. He hadn't got it last time I saw him, maybe four weeks ago.'

Blunt nodded with approval. 'That clears that point up.'

'Clears what point?' I asked.

'Fragments of the cheek and jaw were found,' said Blunt as he turned away, leaving the morgue attendant to cover up the remains of Maitland. 'No traces of a beard.'

Jackson shuddered. 'I wouldn't like to have to go

through that again.'

'You won't have to, Mr Jackson,' said Blunt. 'You've been very helpful. The department appreciates your co-operation.'

'Then you won't be needing me anymore?'

'Only for the inquest,' said Blunt. 'Merely to confirm your identification.'

'The sooner I can forget all about this, the better I'll like it,' shuddered Jackson.

I could sympathise with him. I had the uneasy feeling that the faceless Maitland would project himself into my future nightmares.

Back upstairs in Blunt's office, he once again thanked Jackson, who departed with visible relief.

I settled down opposite Blunt, lit myself a cigarette.

'How did Williams take it?' I asked.

'Like you'd expect him to take it,' he grunted. 'The guy's upset. Said he suspected all the time that his wife was having an affair. But he's taking it badly. Jittery and overwrought.'

'Pathologist's report?' I queried.

'An open-and-shut case,' said Blunt. 'Suicide letter and both of them together with a coupla Mills bombs tied around their necks. What could be clearer?'

'And the pathologist's report?' I persisted.

Blunt drew deeply on his cigarette, carefully tapped ash into the tray. 'Pathologists aren't miracle men.'

'Meaning what?'

His grey eyes stared across the desk into mine. 'Meaning that two bodies exposed to the weather for three weeks decompose. What kinda information do you expect a pathologist to dig up? Flow of blood stopped abruptly. Death occurred instantaneously, and no evidence of abnormal physical ailments. No evidence of existing brain tumours or cancers that were liable to affect the balance of their minds.'

'An open-and-shut case,' I said.

'Yeah,' said Blunt, challengingly.

'So you're changing your tone,' I jeered. 'Just a few days ago you were planning to hang a murder rap around Williams's neck if his wife turned up dead. Right now that doesn't look such a smart idea, does it?'

His steely grey eyes glinted angrily. 'I said two hundred grand was a motive for murder. That's all I said.'

'So Williams is in the clear now?'

'What d'you think?'

I shrugged my shoulders. 'I'm just a reporter,' I said. 'An observer. The river of life flows by and I write about it. Sometimes dramatise it, sometimes soft-pedal. Sometimes I even jump in up to my neck and almost drown myself. But mainly I'm just an observer. I don't set myself up to be a judge.'

His steely grey eyes were glistening. 'Got any special angles?'

I climbed to my feet slowly. 'Nope,' I drawled. 'I can add two and two. A guy who can hypnotise three dames into thinking he's the cat's whiskers, can hypnotise a fourth dame into thinking the same, even though she's married.'

His eyes were still glinting. He said softly: 'I've strung along with you on this, Hank. I've let you in on everything, just so you can see the way the department works. We're not hanging any raps on innocent guys. The inquest will return a verdict of suicide. That wraps it up. That's the way we work. Open and clean. I hope you understand that.'

I moved towards the door. 'Sure I understand,' I said. 'There's just one thing that worries me.'

'Yeah?' He sounded interested, but was too proud to ask directly.

I paused with my hand on the door knob. 'Something that puzzles me,' I said tantalisingly.

He couldn't hold it back. He said curiously: 'What's that, Hank?'

'Just this,' I said. 'How does a Don Juan like John Maitland, with three dames on a string, get so worked up about a dame with two hundred grand clear cash that he wants to commit suicide instead of having the time of his life?'

Blunt asked: 'What are you getting at? What's on your mind, Hank?'

There was nothing on my mind. I just wanted to make Blunt believe I was smarter than I was. Maybe even get him worried a little. I smiled mysteriously, said softly: 'I'll be seeing you, bud,' and slid out quietly, closed the door carefully behind me.

11

I thumbed her door push, kept my thumb on it until she opened up, brown eyes staring at me in reproving surprise that melted into pleasant welcome.

I pushed inside, took off my fedora, skimmed it across the room so it fell on a settee, and climbed out of my slicker.

She hovered around me like a ministering angel, took my coat, carefully hung it on a hanger, then hung it on a hook.

That amused me. I usually dropped my slicker on the floor in a corner.

'I've read all about it,' she said quietly.

'Sure,' I said. 'I wrapped it up for you, honey. John Maitland on a plate. John Maitland in the morgue with no face. John Maitland committing suicide with his girlfriend.'

She stared at me with wide eyes. Something about the way she looked showed I was talking crazily. Maybe I was. In the last twenty-four hours, I'd had a lot of shocks as well as very little rest.

'How about a drink?' I said.

'Yes,' she said quickly. 'Of course. Rye?'

'That'll do.'

I dropped down into a settee, stretched out my legs, fumbled in my pocket for a pack of cigarettes and it lit up carefully.

She brought a glass over to me, placed it in my hand, perched on the edge of the chair facing me, and stared with anxious eyes.

I raised my glass to my lips, sipped, rolled the spirit around my tongue. 'That's good,' I said. 'That's real good. It's just what I needed.'

'I've been reading about it,' she said with bated breath. 'It's just like a dream. I ask what you can do about John Maitland and the next I know, you're writing it up, telling how he was found, describing it like you were there when it happened.'

'You were lucky you didn't see them,' I said hollowly. The memory of the way they had looked, locked together and with their faces blown away, came back at me with the impact of a kick in the solar plexus. I gulped down the contents of the glass, held it out to her empty. 'More,' I said.

Without a word, she took the glass, refilled it at the cocktail cabinet and brought a recharge. She settled down again on the edge of the chair. 'It *was* Maitland?' she asked, with breathless impatience. 'It really was Maitland? You've seen him?'

'Yeah,' I said. 'I've seen him.' And I was remembering it vividly. I took another quick pull at the glass, felt the warmth of the liquor flooding around inside me, spreading a warm, rosy glow that heated my blood and thawed the cold, morbid memories.

'Was it ... so dreadful?'

I looked at her. But it was more than looking. I kinda surveyed her, charted her, ran my eyes over her like they were fingers, sensed the strong, compelling feminine urge inside her, knew she was a woman and was pleased I was a man. That's the way death gets you. It works on your mind, nibbles away at your brain, until you're scared of the future, afraid to put one foot before the other, makes you relish life and living, makes you conscious of your manhood.

She flushed, dropped her eyes. She said quietly: 'I knew I could rely on you. I knew you'd help me … somehow!'

Sure I'd helped. I'd found John Maitland. Again a cold shudder ran down my spine. I gulped at the glass, poured down a shot that sizzled through down to my toes. I stretched out my hand, gave her the empty glass. 'Pour it in, sister,' I said. 'Pour it in.'

She looked at me doubtfully. 'Are you sure?'

'Pour it in,' I growled.

I watched as she went across to the cocktail cabinet. Her dress was tight and her haunches were firm and powerful, stretching the skirt as she tilted the bottle.

'What's the idea?' I demanded thickly. 'I'm watching. Keep tilting that bottle.'

'Do you …?' she faltered.

'Sure I do,' I rasped. 'I've gotta warm up. I've been staring at corpses all day. It takes a hell of a lot of rye to wash corpses out of your system. You wanna try it sometime.'

She poured three fingers. Three thick fingers. I watched with approval as she added only a dash of ginger ale.

Once again she perched herself on the chair opposite me, watched intently as I sipped and rejoiced in the fiery, burning taste of the liquor.

'You've seen him … Hank?' she persisted.

'Yeah, I've seen him,' I said.

'And you're sure it's him?'

'Sure I'm sure,' I said. My toes were tingling. My belly was tingling. My brain was tingling, too. 'Sure,' I said. 'I've seen him. I've seen him twice.' I shook my head sadly. 'He doesn't look so good. Then I frowned at her. She was leaning towards me, brown eyes soulful and sincere. The neat frock she wore was discreetly buttoned at the neck. There was only the tiniest suggestion of a vee neckline. I remembered the way she had been that night, a fragile shoulder-strap slipping down her rounded upper arm. 'You look good, though,' I added. But I didn't say it clearly. The words were like bit, round marbles in my mouth, and the rye was tingling at me brain.

'You're loading yourself, Hank,' she warned.

'That's where you're wrong,' I said. 'I'm warming myself. I've seen them today and they're cold too. Cold as death. They've got cold fingers, rigid arms and no faces. They're stone cold, unsociable. I don't like them around. I've gotta get rid of them. I've gotta warm myself, get so hot I melt them.' My eyes washed over her. 'You're getting me hot too, honey!'

'You've gotta do something for me, Hank.'

'Sure,' I said enthusiastically. 'I'll do something for you. I'll make a job of it, too.'

Her fingers were clenching and unclenching. 'I've gotta be sure. You must understand that. I've gotta be sure. I want to see him.'

I sipped more rye. 'I haven't been sleeping,' I told her seriously. 'Ever since I was here last, I haven't been able to sleep. You've kinda worked yourself deep down inside me. It's got so I can't work, can't sleep. D'you know how it is?'

'Yeah,' she breathed. 'I understand. You've made me understand. But there's this other thing, too. I've gotta get it out of my system. You can help, Hank. I've just gotta be sure. I want to see him.'

I stared at her with wide eyes. 'See who?'

'Maitland,' she said grimly. 'I want to see him. Just to assure myself, to make sure it's really him.'

I drained my glass, peered down into the depths of it. It was empty and blurry. 'Got no face,' I said.

'You could arrange it,' she said fiercely. 'You've got influence. I just can't be happy until I know. I've gotta know. Can't you understand that?' Long, slim fingers curled around my wrists, shook me vigorously. 'You've gotta understand, Hank.'

I let my eyes wash over her. It didn't matter about the vee not being revealing. The firm roundness of her body was convincing enough. 'Sure, honey,' I said thickly. 'I understand. Just you and me. That's the way it is. That's the way it's gotta be. Just you and me. I knew right away, the first time we met.'

'But later, Hank,' she panted. 'Don't you see, I've got to know, I've got to be sure. I owe it to Pat.'

'Listen, kid,' I said. 'This is important.' Then I broke off. I knew it was important, but the important thought eluded me. I searched for it through a warm, clogging fog, found it, grasped it tightly. 'You're important to me,' I announced. 'Right from the time I saw your shoulder-strap slipping down ...' I broke off. Vaguely I realised I was letting up the curtain on that part of my mind I shouldn't allow to become public. I started again.

'Right from the first time I saw you, I've been thinking about you, haven't been able to sleep, haven't been able to work, been thinking about you all the time.'

'Will you do it, Hank?' she pleaded. 'Will you do it?'

'Do what?' I asked vaguely.

'Take me there. Take me there so I can see him.'

I gazed at her, crinkling my brow. Then I stared into my empty glass. It was slowly dawning on me she wanted to go and see him. See that body without a face, see those white, stiff limbs, that caved-in chest and the empty, splintered brain pan.

'You don't wanna do that,' I told her.

Her nails were gouging into my wrists. 'Listen, Hank. You've gotta listen to me. I know it's gonna be awful. It's gonna be shocking. But I've just gotta know. I owe it to Pat. I've just gotta know, and you've gotta take me there. Afterward, Hank, we can think about ourselves. Just you and me. But first I've gotta know.'

I stared at her. The bodice was still firm and rounded, but I could sense it was kinda aloof from me, withdrawn. Like a prize in a fairground that I had to win. 'He's got no face,' I said hollowly. From a distance, I kinda listened to myself laughing. 'He's a Don Juan without a face,' I heard myself say.

'You've gotta take me.' Her voice was cool, hard, and determined.

'I don't wanna see it.' I was getting the craziest impulses. Now I wanted to cry.

'You don't have to. You just take me there.'

'You won't like it,' I said warningly, and looked around expectantly.

She was standing up now, still holding my wrists, drawing me to my feet. 'You don't need any more to drink. You've had too much already. Just hold on a minute while I get my coat.'

My brain was tingling pleasantly; dangerously

pleasantly. 'You won't like it,' I said. 'He's got no face.' Thinking about it made it seem funny. I chuckled loudly. 'He's got no face.'

She was back now, shrugging into her outdoor coat, taking me by the arm. 'I don't say I blame you for getting a skinful,' she said. She urged me towards the door. 'Maybe I'll come back and get a skinful myself.'

'You ain't gonna like it,' I told her. 'A Don Juan without a face. It's tough for a guy who hasn't got a face. Makes it kinda difficult to drink rye.'

'We'll get a taxi,' she said. 'What's the address?'

'Just ask for the morgue,' I told her. 'It's the best hotel in town.' I chuckled. 'If you're cold.'

The guy in charge of the morgue objected to me and Betty viewing his charges. He objected right up to ten bucks. Then, with a beam of satisfaction and the air of a guide at the Tower of London, he led the way downstairs, along the stone corridors to the door of the ice-box.

Betty shuddered when he swung wide the iron door and cold air tainted with the odour of preservative chemicals wafted out to hit us in the face.

It wasn't only the cold that made her shudder. Those two still, white mounds below the white sheets were grisly and gruesome enough to give an undertaker the creeps.

To the guard in charge of that morgue it was just a job. There was a breezy nonchalance in his step as he strode across to the remains of John Maitland, took the end of the sheet in his hand, and made to throw it back.

Then he remembered, poised, switched his eyes around to Betty and gulped.

'Just a minute, miss. This ain't pleasant. You sure you wanna see ...'

'Yes,' she said quickly, in a tight little voice. Her knuckles were gleaming whitely as she clenched her hands.

He looked at me, and I raised my eyebrows, shrugged my shoulders. My brain was tingling only slightly now. Even rye couldn't ward off the depressing coldness of that morgue.

He stood there undecided, gulped, and had another try. 'It's kinda difficult, miss. You see, there ain't no face that you'd recognise, and I don't know that a young lady would wanna see the rest ...'

Betty took a quick step forwards. Her face was white, her eyes glowing. 'Give it to me,' she said thickly. 'Let me do it.' And as she spoke, she was taking the end of the sheet from his unresisting fingers.

'You wanna think twice, miss,' he protested weakly. 'You don't know how ...'

Her face was white and determined. So determined she used maybe more strength than she intended. She stripped it right down off him.

He didn't look any better than he'd looked earlier. The shattered, faceless head was just as shocking. Candidates for a slab in the morgue ain't usually going places, so they don't need clothes. That was another thing that made the stiff, white limbs so shocking. Even more shocking on account of Betty being a dame.

'Let's go,' I said hoarsely. My brain wasn't tingling at all. That cold joint had shocked all the rye out of me.

She stood like a statue, staring down at him. Just staring, staring, staring. It was like she was hypnotised. She stared so long, I began to feel she was as stiff and frozen as he was.

'Listen, kid,' I said. 'You've seen ...'

She gave no warning, no sign it was gonna happen. One moment she was staring, white-faced and rigid, the next moment she was heeling over backwards, stiff like her bones had frozen, not even giving a moan.

I almost didn't catch her. I got my hands up and her shoulders hit them. I took the sudden strain, managed to cushion her fall before her haunches hit the stone floor.

'I warned her,' said the cop dolefully. 'I warned her.'

'Let's get out of here,' I rasped.

I took a firmer grip on her, slipped one arm around her waist, the other under her thighs. I hefted her, carried her out through the morgue doors.

He re-draped Maitland with the white sheet, slammed and locked the morgue doors and followed me along the stone corridors.

'I warned her,' he said again, like he was trying to excuse himself. 'That ain't the kinda thing a young dame should see.'

'Cut on ahead,' I said tersely. Dig up a shot to brandy from somewhere.'

Upstairs, seated in an interviewing office, it took three or four minutes of wrist slapping, forehead rubbing and brandy feeding to bring her round.

Her brown eyes stared up at mine, haunted and tortured. 'I didn't know ...' she faltered. 'Everything just went black.'

'I warned you,' said the guard dolefully.

'It wasn't a pleasant sight,' I told her. I noticed her cheeks had a greyish tinge.

She started to climb to her feet. I pushed her back. 'Take it easy.'

'I'm all right,' she protested.

'Maybe you think you are. You've just had a bad shock.'

'I'm all right,' she insisted. Her face was drawn, but once again that streak of determination or obstinacy inside her was asserting itself.

'Just a coupla minutes more then,' I compromised.

'I just wanna get out of here.'

The guard shrugged his shoulders as though to say, 'All dames are the same. They can't be reasoned with.' Then he turned away, went down to the far end of the office, tucked the bottle of brandy back in a lower drawer.

Her eyes caught mine, urgent and compelling. She leaned forward towards me, and I knew what she wanted, lowered my head so she could whisper. 'Let's get out of here,' she said hoarsely. 'There's something you've gotta know.'

'All right,' I said. 'We'll go in a minute.'

'You've gotta know this,' she panted. 'You've gotta know it. That guy in there. He's not John Maitland. He's not John Maitland at all!'

12

We went to a bar just along the road and I brought her another brandy, ordered a rye for myself.

'How d'you know he's not John Maitland?' I asked. I figured the shock musta been too much for her, upset her judgment.

'I know,' she said quietly. 'I know it's not him.'

'Feminine instinct?' I jeered.

'If you like,' she said.

'Your instinct won't stand up,' I said. 'The guy's been identified. He was living in Chicago with a fella named Jackson. Did you notice those moles Maitland had on his arm? He was identified by those.'

Her brown eyes were staring into mine. 'There must be something fishy about Jackson,' she said with finality. 'He's made a false identification.'

'Listen, kid,' I said gently. 'You're just a little upset, and …'

'Where does Jackson live?' she interrupted.

'Now you wanna see him, huh?'

Her eyes were level and disconcertingly honest. 'That's right,' she agreed. 'I wanna see Jackson.'

'You won't be happy until you see him?'

'You've tuned in on my wavelength, Hank.'

'All right,' I said wearily. 'Just hold on.'

I went to a telephone kiosk, rang police headquarters and got Jackson's address. There was no telephone to his apartment, so I rang through to the janitor, was told Jackson was out.

'Any idea where I might contact him?'

'I expect you'll find him at the Duberry,' the janitor told me.

The Duberry was a sporting club where you could buy drinks most times of the day. I rang there and the reception desk said: 'Yes, sir. Mr Jackson is here. If you'll hold on, I'll get him for you.'

'Never mind,' I told her. 'I'll come right over.'

When I got back to the counter, Betty had finished her brandy. She raised one eyebrow enquiringly.

'Okay,' I said wearily. 'We'll take a cab and make you happy. We'll be there in fifteen minutes.'

'You're a real nice guy,' she said softly.

The way she said it was encouraging. It reminded me of how she could yield when she wanted. The mental picture of a fragile shoulder-strap edged back into my mind. When we climbed into a taxi, I put my arm around her.

She leaned against me.

I pressed my cheek against hers, felt the soft touch of her hair, smelt the sweet cleanliness of her in my nostrils. 'You're a nice kid,' I said.

'You're nice too, Hank,' she said softly. There was a note of regret in her voice. 'The trouble is, Hank, I'm kinda all screwed up inside. It's like I can't be myself, can't respond naturally. It's getting me, Hank. All the time, I'm thinking about Pat, the torment she endured, and knowing about this other thing, and wanting to find

Maitland.'

'What other thing?' I said sharply.

'You wouldn't understand,' she said dully. 'You wouldn't understand.'

She was close to me, touching me from hip to ankle. That memory of that slipping shoulder-strap kept edging into my brain, and the closeness of her was making the memory more vivid. I moved my hand and she sighed, leaned closer against me.

'What are we just playing for?' I rasped. 'You know the way it is. Both of us feeling the same. Why do you ...'

She'd turned towards me, her arms up and around my neck as she strained against me. Her lips were hot, moist and searching, her hair soft and silky, her fingers cool and thrilling.

After a time, I panted warningly: 'We're almost there!'

Reluctantly she broke away from me, sank back into the darker corner of the cab.

'You witch,' I panted. 'You'll drive me crazy that way.'

I heard the rustle of clothing as she buttoned.

'I didn't know it could be this way,' she panted. 'I've never before ...' Her voice trailed off.

'It's just something that happens,' I said hoarsely. 'A guy and a dame together!'

'And you, Hank,' she whispered. 'You're happy?'

'Honey,' I panted. 'We've had no time. I want to *really* know you. Everything about you. I wanna have you close, really close for a good long time.'

'Later, Hank,' she whispered. 'Later, when I'm not screwed up inside and ...'

The taxi was drawing into the kerb. 'Are you

okay?' I interrupted. 'We get out here.'

'Yes, I'm okay.'

I paid off the driver while she climbed out. Her face wasn't white any longer. It was kinda flushed and alive. Her eyes were sparkling too. She took my arm when we pushed through the swing doors of the Duberry Club.

I saw Jackson right away. He was perched on a high stool at the bar, quietly contented, smoking a cigarette and sipping a highball.

Betty's fingers gouged my arm. 'Is that him?' she breathed, following the direction of my gaze.

'Yeah,' I said. 'That's Jackson.'

She kept her eyes fastened on him as we walked over to him. Just before we reached him, she said in a whisper: 'Remember. My name's not Scott. It's Tanner. Betty Tanner.'

I didn't get the chance to ask where she got that cloak and dagger stuff. Jackson glanced towards me at that moment. His eyes rested on me, stared and then lighted up with recognition.

I walked forward, extended my hand. 'Hello,' I said. 'You can buy us a drink.' I half turned. 'Let me introduce my friend. Betty ...'

'Betty Tanner,' she interrupted quickly. Then she said slowly and deliberately, giving me a cue to follow: 'What a coincidence. No sooner do we casually drop in to have a drink than Hank meets someone he knows.'

I gulped.

'It's a pleasure,' said Jackson. 'What will you have? A Martini? Highball?'

'Martini, please.'

'Make mine a rye,' I said.

I tried to catch Betty's eye. She deliberately

avoided looking at me, like she knew my eyes were asking her questions she didn't wanna answer. I didn't like the way she was watching Jackson, either; staring at him intently, running her eyes over him, examining him closely. It was occurring to me that Jackson was the kinda guy any dame would look at. He was tall and he was handsome, and apart from his crew-cut, his fair hair was soft and silken. The kinda hair dames love to touch.

The bartender brought our drinks.

I said: 'I guess Betty would like to know a few things about ...'

She flashed me a swift warning glance that Jackson couldn't see, interrupted gently but firmly: 'I'm a stranger to town. I'm an old friend of Hank, and he's showing me around.'

'You've got the right guy to show you around,' said Jackson. 'Mr Janson is a guy who gets around everywhere.' He smiled at me genially. 'Nice stunt that telepathy act.'

I raised my eyebrows. 'Stunt?' I objected. 'If that's a trick, I'll eat my hat.'

'I read about it this afternoon,' he said. 'They really pulled it off, didn't they?'

'Excellent show,' I told him. 'Completely mystifying.'

'What's gone wrong with everything then?'

I stared at him. 'Nothing's gone wrong with it.'

He stared back. 'Then what are you doing here? Aren't you ...'

It hit me then. I glanced at the clock on the wall with sudden alarm. In just ten minutes I was due on the stage at the Casino, announcing the correctness of Los Guitanos's prophecy.

'Hell,' I gulped. 'I'd clean forgotten. I've gotta go.

I've gotta be on stage making an announcement in ten minutes. Drink up and we'll get cracking.'

Betty kinda hung back. She said coldly: 'It's all right, Hank. You go right ahead. As soon as you're through, come straight back. I'll be waiting for you.' She smiled up at Jackson. 'I'm sure I'll have good company.'

I stared at her. I glared at Jackson and saw the conceited smile tugging at his lips.

'You're coming too,' I rasped.

'I'll wait, Hank,' she said gently. 'We've been running around so much I'm exhausted. I'll wait for you.'

I breathed hard. 'Okay,' I growled angrily. 'If that's the way you want it.' I nodded at Jackson. 'Be seeing you.' I glared at Betty. 'Don't get lost.'

'Look after yourself, Hank,' she said sweetly. 'Don't trip over your words.'

I walked out fuming, with the memory of her slipping shoulder-strap a background to the softness of her eyes. I flagged a taxi, climbed aboard and offered him ten bucks to get me to the Casino within ten minutes.

He earned those ten bucks. It was the most scarifying ride of my life. I puffed into the theatre as Billy's act was drawing to an end. I walked swiftly down the aisle at the side, reached the foot of the steps leading to the stage as the manager stepped to the microphone and announced that a representative of the *Chronicle* was in the theatre to make a statement.

I panted up on to the stage, sweating, hot and uncomfortable. I advanced to the microphone, took up my position between Billy and Lucy and waited for the applause to die away.

I was mad at Betty. She'd got me all steamed up in

the taxi, and seeing the way she was looking at Jackson roused inside me the anger of jealousy. There'd been real, genuine interest in her eyes when she had looked at Jackson.

It was that knowledge and the nearness of Lucy that made me watch her with sideways glances while I waited for the applause to die away.

Right then, Lucy had the same effect upon me as when I'd last seen her. And the last time I'd seen her I'd been dreaming. Those slender, silken strands of black were even more slender than I remembered, her curves more prominent and fascinating than I'd believed possible.

I became acutely conscious that silence was awaiting me. From behind me, the manager cleared his throat noisily. Thousands of pairs of eyes were watching me watching Lucy.

I flushed like a beetroot, tore my eyes away from Lucy, stepped forward and took a firm grip on the microphone to help get a grip on myself. I said slowly but clearly:

'Ladies and gentlemen. On behalf of the *Chicago Chronicle*, it is my privilege to describe to you the results of one of the most rigidly and severely supervised tests ever imposed upon a clairvoyant.'

13

It took a whole lot longer to explain than I'd reckoned. I couldn't use just a coupla brief sentences. I had to explain how the test had been proposed without Billy or Lucy having knowledge of it, and describe the steps taken to guard the envelope right up until the moment it was opened.

Then Billy had a few words to say, then Lucy, and finally the manager. In all, it was maybe three quarters of an hour before I could get off the stage. And all the time, I was on thorns, because I was thinking of Betty looking at me, and not wanting to leave her with that fair-headed Romeo.

As the curtain fell, I made my way quickly through the wings to the stage door. 'You got a telephone?' I asked.

'Help yourself,' said the doorkeeper.

I put through a call to the Duberry Club. 'There's a young lady with Mr Jackson,' I said. 'Would you tell her Mr Janson is on his way? He'll be there in fifteen minutes.'

Her cool, clear voice was emotionless and disinterested. 'I'm sorry, sir. Mr Jackson is no longer here. He left some time ago.'

My heart missed a coupla beats. 'You're sure?'

'Yes, sir,' she said. 'I'm sure.'

My mouth was dry. 'The young lady is still there?'

'They left together.'

My voice was so dry I could hardly get the words out. 'Was any message left for me?'

'No, sir. No messages.'

I replaced the receiver and scowled at the doorkeeper. He stared back with a hurt look in his eyes.

'To hell with her,' I snarled.

'Beg pardon?' he asked.

'Forget it,' I gritted. 'Just thinking aloud.'

'Having trouble, sir?'

'Yeah,' I said bitterly. 'The usual kind. Woman trouble.'

He nodded his head understandingly. 'I'm a married man myself.'

I fumbled in my pocket for a cigarette. *'The hell of it,'* I was thinking. And in the same moment I was seeing that fragile, slipping shoulder-strap. Ten minutes with that guy and she'd gone off with him. Left me flat! Anger, resentment and bitterness began to glow inside me. After all, I wasn't unattractive to dames. In fact some dames found me plenty interesting. I wasn't dependent on Betty. Again a momentary mind picture of a slipping shoulder-strap, and the warm, intimate surge of desire inside me.

There were other dames. Sure. There were other dames. I didn't have to depend on Betty. There were dames everywhere. There was one right here in this theatre.

Just thinking about Lucy made me feel a whole lot better. I pulled a dollar bill from my pocket, handed it to the doorkeeper. 'Buy yourself a drink,' I invited. I was suddenly almost happy.

He grabbed and slipped it into his pocket like he'd never got his paws on a dollar bill before. 'Hope everything works out all right,' he said.

'It will,' I said with easy assurance. 'It will.'

I found my way to Billy's dressing room, knuckled the panels.

'Come in,' invited his rich, baritone voice.

I went in, my eyes flickering from Billy seated before his dressing-table mirror to the slender silken strap hanging over the screen. One slim white hand momentarily appeared, and I warmed inside as I pictured her climbing into flimsy, intimate undergarments.

'Pleased you're here,' greeted Billy enthusiastically. 'Grab yourself a chair and sit down.'

I sat down. I kept watching the screen.

'Did we knock them, fella?' boasted Billy. 'Did we really knock them?'

'You sure did,' I said.

I was still watching the screen when Lucy came around from back of it. Her blue eyes smiled a welcome as she clip-clopped across to her dressing-table, sat down and began to do things to her face. Her shoes did something for her. They were high-heeled and set off her figure when she walked, so that her natural curves seemed taut, strong and irresistible.

'Hiya, Lucy,' I greeted.

Her blue eyes came around to mine, smiled softly and invitingly. 'You've been awfully good to us, Mr Hank Janson,' she said softly. Just the sound of her voice made my toes curl. The scanty undergarment was already making my hair curl.

'That was worth ten grand's worth of publicity,' said Billy with satisfaction.

'What about it, Lucy?' I asked breathlessly. 'May I take you to dinner tonight?'

'We can count on top billing in every State,' said Billy happily.

'What d'you say, Billy?' Lucy asked.

'D'you have to ask this monkey?' I demanded.

She flushed slightly, a tiny smile tugging at her lips. 'I rely on Billy for a great many things.'

'Hank's okay, honey,' said Billy disinterestedly. 'You two push off, buy yourself a nice dinner some place. He's a wolf right enough. But he's a tame wolf. Just once in a while you have to beat him down with a baseball bat. But apart from that, he's not a bad guy.'

'D'you mind waiting for me, Mr Janson?' she asked, and her blue eyes were soft and trusting. 'I shan't be long getting ready.'

'Sure I'll wait,' I said. Watching her get ready was no penance. On the contrary, it was a real pleasure. 'Call me Hank,' I suggested.

'Okay, Hank,' she said in her husky, intimate voice that started my toes curling all over again.

'Kidding on one side, Hank,' said Billy. 'I'm really grateful to you. Today's the turning point in our career.'

'Just tell me one thing, will you, Billy?' I grinned. 'How d'you do it?'

He turned around slowly to face me, his eyes widening, his face expressing surprise. 'What d'ya mean, Hank? Fix it?'

'A few days ago,' I reminded him, 'you were packing your bags. You reckoned you were finished, told me your act was one hundred percent trick. You said I'd fixed a test you couldn't beat in a month of Sundays. But somehow you've done it. Somehow you've pulled off the impossible. You know you can trust me. I won't talk. I just wanna know how you did it.'

His brow crinkled. 'Let's get this straight, Hank. When we had that little chat a few days ago, you didn't really believe I was serious, did you? I was only ribbing, you know. Me and Lucy have never been worried. Right from the beginning we knew we'd be proved right.'

Lucy climbed to her feet, reached for sheer stockings, began to pull them over her long, shapely, fascinating legs. I tried to watch her and Billy at the same time. 'You sounded serious the other day,' I said. 'You got me real worried, thinking I'd smashed your act.'

He chuckled softly, showing his amusement. 'What d'you think of that, Lucy?' he chuckled. 'We actually fooled Hank when we told him it was a trick. He *really* believed it was trickery.'

She smiled back, showed white teeth, reached for a flimsy, frothy and tantalising garment that she clipped tight around her waist, strained taut the transparent stockings.

'How do you think we can convince him?' she asked.

'Maybe you'd like to test us on next week's headlines, Hank,' suggested Billy hopefully.

I looked at him. I looked at Lucy. 'It isn't possible,' I said uncertainly. 'Nobody can see into the future.'

'Lucy can,' said Billy with finality.

'Can you really see into the future, Lucy?' I asked sincerely, almost pleadingly.

She reached for a thin frock, pulled it over her head. 'Of course I can. I can even foresee what's going to happen tonight.' There was a mischievous twinkle in her blue eyes, as she buttoned her bodice, fastened the zip at the side. The dress fitted her like a glove, strained smoothly taut across her thighs, faithfully followed every line of her youthful curves.

Billy's expressive eyes stared at me sincerely. 'I'm warning you, Hank. She's no pushover to take on a dinner date. She knows what you're thinking about almost before you start thinking it for yourself.'

A shy, pleased smile touched Lucy's lips as she saw the way I was looking at her. 'She doesn't have to be a mind-reader to know what I'm thinking,' I told him.

'Neither do I,' said Billy, chuckling.

'If you'll get my wrap for me, Hank, I'll be ready almost at once,' she said.

It was a short, fur wrap, and as I placed it around her shoulders I fancied she leaned back against me.

'Have a good time,' wished Billy. 'I'll be seeing you.'

She was the kinda dame any guy would be proud to be seen out with. But I didn't want to show her off. I wanted to have her for myself. So I took her to a quiet, intimate kinda joint for dinner, spent most of the time I was talking to her across the dinner-table staring at her bodice, and most of the time on the dance floor straining her tight against me.

But there was something intangible about her. She wasn't playing hard to get or holding me off to whet my appetite. On the dance floor she didn't exactly melt against me, either. Dark suspicion grew and lingered deep down at the back of my brain.

'Give me the low-down, kid,' I rasped. 'I'm not a Mrs Grundy. I just wanna know where I stand. Is there anything between you and Billy?'

Her blue eyes stared at me. Then a smile rippled across her lips. A really amused smile. 'Good heavens, no,' she said. 'What on earth makes you think that!'

There were a lot of things made me think it. But no dame would have the face to lie so brazenly. And if things were that way between her and Billy, he'd be crazy to let her go out with me.

'Just a crazy hunch,' I said.

'You're a nice, crazy kinda guy, Hank,' she said softly, gently and invitingly.

It could be she was naturally shy. Maybe too shy to be rushed. I said tentatively: 'Kinda hot in here, isn't it? What say we get outside, get some fresh air?'

'Anything you want, Hank.'

I paid the bill and we went out into the cool night air. A taxi was cruising past and I flagged it into the kerbside.

'Where to?' asked the driver.

There were lots of places I could think of. Coffee in my apartment, for example. But I didn't want to rush her. I looked at her, raised one eyebrow enquiringly. 'Where to, honey?'

She coulda said: 'Anywhere you say, honey.' She coulda even said: 'I leave it to you.'

She didn't.

She said: 'I don't know what your plans are.'

'Get in, anyway,' I said gruffly.

'Where to?' repeated the driver.

'Just drive around,' I told him. 'Just drive around until we work up ideas.'

In the intimate darkness of the taxi there was a chance we could work up quite an idea. Maybe even work out that going to my apartment was a first class idea.

I sat down beside her, thrilled at the touch of her. I took her cool, slim fingers in mine. She giggled.

'What's so funny?' I snarled angrily.

'After what Billy warned me about you, I never expected to find you so timid.'

'Timid!' That one challenging word swept away my reticence.

'Maybe I can do better this way,' I said, and put my arm around her shoulders, pulled her close.

She was warm and snuggly, that thin frock so smooth it felt like skin. She was chuckling deliciously. 'You're quite a guy, aren't you, Hank?'

It coulda been my imagination I fancied I could detect merriment and mockery in her voice.

'And you're quite a dame,' I said.

She took my wrist, held it tightly. 'Don't take too much for granted, Hank,' she whispered.

I'd seen her climb into that frock. I knew just how little she wore beneath it. Knowing that, the nearness of her became intoxicating and heady. 'You get me,' I panted. 'You do things to me.'

'Don't be naughty,' she admonished calmly.

'There's no harm in it,' I insisted.

'But I don't want!'

I tried to kiss her, and in the darkness she twisted her face away quickly, chuckling when I missed, nuzzling her ear instead. 'Naughty,' she admonished again.

'You scared?'

'Would I be here if I was scared?'

'This time don't run away.'

'I don't think I should let you kiss me.' Her voice was artificially prim.

'What the hell,' I growled. 'There's nothing in kissing.' I was thinking: *Sure, that's right. There's nothing in kissing. It's what it sometimes leads to!*

'Are you sure of that, Hank?' she asked, curiosity in her voice.

'Sure, I'm sure.'

'You act like you know how to kiss,' she breathed invitingly.

This time she didn't twist away. Her lips met mine, sweet-tasting lips, warm and lingering, hot and alive with movement. It was a kiss that sent fiery trailers spurting right through to the tips of my toes, a kiss that revived my dream memories with a vividness that made me weak. I wanted her.

I wanted her so bad I couldn't wait.

She twisted her lips away abruptly, and this time she was holding my wrist with both hands.

'All right, Hank,' she panted. 'That's it. That's enough.'

'What d'ya mean, enough!' I asked quickly.

'There's no harm in a kiss,' she said breathlessly. 'That's what you said.'

I had to wait for my heart to slow down before I could ask hoarsely: 'What are you trying to do? Drive me crazy?'

'No, Hank,' she said softly. 'You're doing that yourself.'

'What's the matter with you?'

'I just don't want, Hank. I told you that before.'

'Are you different or something?'

She was still panting. But there was a chuckle in her voice. 'I hope not. It's just that my husband wouldn't like it.'

'Your husband!' It was like a blow between the eyes. 'Your husband!' I said again, disbelievingly.

'Maybe he wouldn't even like me kissing,' she said. 'But you were so keen on it, and you said there was nothing in it.'

I let go of her, fumbled in my pocket for my handkerchief so I could wipe my sweating palms. I was like a guy tortured by thirst, who's had a pannikin of water pulled from his reach.

'How d'you like that,' I panted. 'You're married!'

That dark, lingering suspicion reared inside me.

'What's your husband think about Billy?' I rasped.

'We're kinda related in a way,' she said calmly. 'Billy married my sister. That makes him my brother-in-law. And since my husband is Billy's cousin, we're a pretty close-knit family.'

'You shoulda told me,' I gulped. 'I figured that ...'

There was a note of regret in her voice. 'Has this made you feel bad, Hank?'

'What do you think?' I snarled bitterly.

'I'm sorry,' she said sincerely. She reached out, pressed my hand sympathetically. 'You know, you're really quite a nice guy. Maybe if I'd have met you earlier ...'

'You were giving me the run-around amusing yourself,' I accused.

'I wasn't,' she said. Sincerity was in her voice. 'You invited me to dinner. I was pleased to accept. You had no right to expect ...'

She was right there. Maybe I wouldn't have expected anything if Betty – *shoulder-strap slipping, revealing firmly rounded curves* – hadn't got me so sore.

'I was gonna invite you to my apartment for a coffee,' I said. 'I figure it wouldn't work out now.'

Again her hand squeezed mine. 'It's better not, Hank. After all, it's like I told you. I'm not different from other girls. I couldn't be sure of myself all the time. Especially in your apartment!'

When she said that, it made me feel better, soothed my wounded pride. 'Where d'you want we should go then, honey?'

'Let's not play with fire,' she said regretfully. 'Take me back to my hotel.'

I sighed, yet deep down inside me I knew it was the best suggestion. 'Pity,' I said regretfully and ruefully. 'I make such good coffee.'

I leaned forward, spoke into the speaking-tube, gave the driver the address.

I went upstairs to her room with her, kinda hovered uncomfortably on one foot. She watched me with amusement shining in her wide blue eyes.

'It's been a pleasure, Lucy,' I said awkwardly.

'For me too,' she said. 'A kinda poignant pleasure.' She held out slim, cool fingers, so I could take them. 'It makes one wonder how things would have worked out if we'd met some time ago.'

'You're a nice kid, Lucy,' I said sincerely.

'I'm clairvoyant,' she said, with a twinkle in her clear blue eyes.

'You're still cute.'

'You're wondering if you might kiss me again?'

'That's like stoking the furnace when there's no water in the boiler. It's liable to result in an explosion.'

She leaned forward impulsively, brushed her lips across my cheek and lips. 'It's been a nice evening,' she breathed.

'It could have been nicer.'

'Don't tempt me,' she said. 'Why don't you go say goodnight to Billy? Leave me now, before I start forgetting my good resolutions.'

'I'll be seeing you, kid.'

I waited until she'd closed the door behind her,

giving me a tiny wistful smile. Then I shrugged my shoulders, smiled ruefully and knuckled the panels of Billy's door.

'Come in,' Billy's rich, baritone voice invited.

He was lying on the bed in his dressing-gown, smoking a cigar and reading through the bunch of newspapers which featured his *dramatic, amazing performance!*

He grinned at me wisely, raised one eyebrow.

'Back early!' he mocked.

'Yep,' I growled, and sprawled myself in an easy chair.

'Nothing doing, huh?'

'Your sister-in-law!' I snarled. 'And married!'

'Maybe I shoulda warned you.'

'It's okay,' I said wearily. 'Every dame I meet doesn't have to be nice on account I get headlines.'

'She's a nice kid,' he said. 'Her husband's a nice guy, too. It's good to have a wife you can trust.'

Maybe it was. For the husband! It didn't make me feel any better. I had two dames constantly on my mind. One of them wouldn't play, and the other had drifted off with a fair-haired Romeo. Both those dames had got me hotter than a chestnut on a brazier, and I was feeling restless. Uncomfortably restless. This was one more night I wasn't gonna sleep easy. And I'd had little enough sleep these past few days at that!

I climbed to my feet, fumbled in my pocket for a cigarette, restlessly paced the floor.

His wise eyes stared at me. 'Feeling frustrated, huh?'

'Are you kidding?' I snarled.

He sat up, swung his legs around off the bed. 'All right, Hank,' he admitted. 'I shouldn't have done it. I shoulda warned you. Especially since I owe you something on account of the publicity. So I'll try and level up. I'll let you in on something.'

I shook my head determinedly. 'Forget it,' I said. 'Little black books with call-girl numbers are not for me. I like genuine affection. I don't like to buy it.'

'You're way off beam,' he said. 'Dames wasn't what I had in mind.'

The note in his rich voice got home at me. I turned around, looked at him levelly. His eyes were holding mine, compelling me to keep looking at him.

'You promise to keep what I'm gonna tell you under your hat?'

'What are you gonna tell me?'

'You promise first,' he said. 'When I've retired, you can use the information if you want. But until then, you don't give to a living soul.'

I began to see what he was getting at. 'You mean ...'

'That's right,' he said. 'I'll give it if you'll promise.'

I was breathing hard. 'You can trust me,' I said. 'I won't use it ever.'

'Not until I've retired, at any rate.'

'Rely on me.'

He took a deep breath. 'You got any idea at all how it was done, Hank? Everyone saw Lucy write that headline on the envelope, and from that moment until the envelope was opened in your office, neither Lucy nor me came within yards of it. Yet it was a pure trick, Hank. Can you figure it out?'

'I've gone crazy trying to figure it.'

He shook his head, chuckled tantalisingly. 'It had me beat too. Right up until a coupla days beforehand, it had beaten me. This act means everything to Lucy and me. I wasn't willing to see it break up without putting up a struggle. That meant taking a chance. And I took a chance. A very long shot. I was lucky. It came off.'

'I'll never figure it.'

He lay back on the bed, stretched his legs comfortably, drew on his cigar and blew smoke towards the ceiling. 'I figured it from all angles,' he said. 'I saw the way it could be done. But it was chancy. Remember when I came down to the Chicago offices?'

'You were watched all the time.'

'Sure,' he said with satisfaction. 'But that was a clean visit. There was nothing phoney about it. But those letters of recommendation your Chief gave me to other newspapers were useful. I used them, went around, got to know reporters and photographers. I was taking a long chance, but it was all or nothing. I got real friendly with one of those photographers. He had a wife and three kids, was shabbily dressed and could obviously use a few extra bucks.' He paused, drew on his cigar again.

I was fidgety with impatience. 'Gwan,' I encouraged. 'G'wan.'

'I bought that photographer for a hundred bucks,' he said with satisfaction. 'It made him happy and made me happy. I spent a coupla hours rehearsing him, showing him exactly what he had to do. Then from that time onwards it was up to him.'

I shook my head sadly. 'I still don't get it.'

He looked at me, grinned irrepressibly. 'And you're supposed to be a smart guy!'

'You'll have to draw a picture. I still can't figure it.'

'You could figure it easily enough if you could see it from the right angle. But you're hypnotised like the audience was hypnotised, Hank. You're still looking at it from the angle of *'How did Lucy know in advance what the headlines were to be'*. That's the wrong angle.'

'What other angle is there?'

He grinned happily. 'Remember the tall, lanky photographer who manoeuvred you into position so he could take a photograph of you with the envelope in the background?'

'Sure,' I said.

'Remember how later he placed the envelope in your hand so he could photograph it?'

I stared at him blankly. 'I still don't get it.'

'Substitution,' he said gently. 'A tall, lanky guy with big hands. Large hands big enough to conceal the substitute envelope, an envelope already prepared that morning with the correct headline, sealed with fancy tapes and placed between two duplicate pieces of glass.'

I gaped at him.

He nodded happily. 'Yeah, Hank. That's how it was done. Just simple substitution. And all the time, everyone was watching me, trying to watch any smart move *I* might try and pull.'

I was breathless. Of all the cool cheek …!

'D'you blame me, Hank?' he pleaded. 'It was all or bust. Only showmanship pulled it off. All that rigmarole of the observers and locking the envelope in the safe, and all the insistence that Lucy was clairvoyant, distracted everyone's attention from the basic factor. And the basic factor was substitution, Hank. Maybe I coulda done it myself, made an excuse to examine the envelope. But it was cleaner paying that photographer a hundred bucks. And folks maybe would have been watching me too closely anyway.'

'Of all the cool cheek!' I said again.

'I owed it to you, Hank,' he said. 'I just had to tell

you.'

I grinned at him. 'You old humbug.'
He grinned back. 'Just a matter of substitution!'

14

Can a guy help being human? Can a guy help his reflexes, his conditioned reactions and his physical impulses?

When I left Billy's hotel, I started walking home. Those two dames went home with me, one either side of me, invisible to everyone but myself, but as provoking and as tantalising and as frustrating as if they'd been there in the flesh.

I was a third of the way home, walking fast, before I realised that walking fast wasn't helping. I just wouldn't be able to rest at home. Meanwhile my physical impulses were goading me into desire for action of some kind.

Lucy was out. Clearly and finally Lucy was out. Even if she changed her attitude, it wouldn't be right, wouldn't be the way I wanted it.

I pushed my way into a drug-store, thumbed nickels into the telephone box and rang the Duberry.

I drew a blank. Jackson hadn't returned.

As far as I knew, Betty hadn't a telephone. But I could catch a taxi over to her apartment!

I was on the sidewalk, waiting for a taxi, when it

struck me I was only five minutes' walk from where Jackson lived. In my present mood, I was ready for anything. Maybe it would be better that way, seeing Jackson first and learning just how things stood between him and Betty.

It was a middle-class block of apartments and I found his name on the downstairs board, walked past a shirt-sleeved janitor who sat down in the passageway and didn't even raise his eyes, climbed to the third floor and walked along the corridor to Apartment 6B.

I noticed the door wasn't even properly closed. I hovered with my thumb poised inches from the push; then I jutted my jaw, leaned my shoulder against the door and found myself staring down a dark passage to light shining from a half-open door at the far end.

I didn't make any secret I was there. Slowly and deliberately I walked down the corridor, my steps loud on the linoleum. I knuckled the panels of the lounge door, pushed it open and kinda framed myself in the doorway.

If Jackson was surprised, he didn't show it. He was settled back in an easy chair and wearing his dressing-gown. Smoke curled upwards from his cigarette, and a half-empty bottle of rye stood on the table beside him. His face showed only mild interest.

'I guess I left the door open,' he commented. 'I'm always doing that.'

I closed the door of the lounge behind me, leaned my shoulders against it and glanced around the room. A half-open door leading off coulda led to the bedroom. Another closed door to the left seemed to mock me. I allowed my eyes to rove on around the room. On the sideboard was a handbag I recognised as Betty's. Bitterness burned inside me, and my lip curled. I nodded towards the half-open door. 'Is that your bedroom?' I snarled.

His eyes showed mild surprise. 'That's right.'

'Is she in here?' I gritted.

A slow, conceited smile crossed his lips. 'No,' he said. 'She's not in there now.' He nodded towards the closed door. 'She's gone through to the bathroom.'

I kept my shoulders pressed against the door. I fumbled in my pocket, drew out a cigarette, placed it to my lips with shaking fingers. I'd never felt so emotionally jarred before. I was aching for a little affection, and instead I was having my nose rubbed into the knowledge that I'd been passed up for this bone-headed crew-cut.

'Sit down,' he invited. 'Make yourself at home.'

'You didn't waste any time,' I snarled.

'I didn't have to,' he said. He was smiling genially, quietly and comfortably at ease. He wouldn't have sat there so complacently if he'd known just how close he was to being torn out of his chair and his nose punched so hard he could use it for a back collar stud.

The anger inside me was sullen and slumbering. Maybe right then I wanted to be goaded, anger to swell up inside me like an overpowering flame. I said aggressively: 'You were supposed to wait for me to come back.'

His eyes widened. 'Now listen, fella,' he said mildly. 'Don't get me wrong. I wasn't horning in. Not waiting for you was the dame's idea. That was the way *she* wanted it..' He gave me a man-to-man grin. 'After all, when a dame puts on pressure, a guy's gotta string along. He just can't help himself.'

I felt murderous, trembling all over, my fists clenched into bone hammers. I wanted to pound his conceited face, punch and pound again and again until all the bitterness had burned out of me. Yet a small voice of reason inside me was holding me back, forcing me to think clearly, making me understand I had no rights over Betty, that she was a free agent and could choose her own company.

'That's kinda hard to believe,' I said dangerously.

'Kinda hard to prove, too. Dames are funny that way. Maybe she wouldn't be anxious to admit it.'

I drew a deep breath, knew my lips were curling back from my teeth. In another coupla seconds I wasn't gonna be able to restrain myself. I was gonna stride across the room, seize him by the throat.

And at that moment I heard the handle of the closed door rattle. I jerked round quickly, faced it, was waiting when she pushed the door open, walked through it and then stopped abruptly, stared at me with shocked and guilty eyes.

Maybe she'd have scuttled back if she'd had the chance. Maybe she would have lied, denied and given me a convincing line. But as she stood there in the doorway, everything was starkly clear and beyond misunderstanding.

She was wearing just a slip, the twin of the one I'd already seen her wearing. Her skin was kinda damp and glowing from the shower, and she was barefooted.

I stared at her. She stared back. Slowly she flushed and then dropped her eyes. She said quietly, guiltily: 'You should have warned me he had come.'

'He's only just arrived,' said Jackson coolly. The satisfied smile of conceit touched his lips. 'Hadn't you better get dressed, honey? You're embarrassing Mr Janson, maybe.'

She bit her lip and, without looking at either

Jackson or myself, padded swiftly to the bedroom. She closed the door carefully behind her. When I looked back at Jackson, his eyes were watching me intently, mockingly. 'Does she act like a dame who's here against her will?' he asked.

She opened the door of the bedroom, thrust her head through. She said in a shamed voice: 'Mr Janson. Will you wait for me, please? I'll only be a few minutes.'

My lip curled. 'Why should I wait for you!'

'Will you take me home, please?'

My eyes glittered at her, switched to Jackson. 'He's been taking care of you so far, hasn't he?'

Jackson said easily: 'I'm kinda tired, ready for bed. You can drop the dame off on your way home, can't you?'

'Please, Hank,' she said.

'Go jump in the lake,' I growled.

'I've an explanation to make you,' she said. 'Please wait.' She closed the door before I could refuse again.

Jackson grinned at me shamelessly. 'You handle dames wrong,' he said. 'You've gotta be tough with them, contemptuous of them. That's the kinda treatment they go for. That's when they just can't do enough for you.'

I clenched my teeth, said nothing. I was feeling like hell, wretched and miserable. But she'd asked me to take her home, and I'd do it. I'd do it so I could show how bitter and contemptuous I felt.

'Help yourself to a drink,' he invited.

'No thanks,' I gritted.

He shrugged his shoulders. 'Sit down. Make yourself at home.'

'I prefer to stand.'

He shrugged his shoulders. 'I'm doing my best to

be sociable, fella.'

'That's okay. You go ahead. I just don't feel sociable.'

The seconds ticked by slowly.

'Sure you won't have a drink?'

'For Chrissakes leave me alone, will ya?'

Again he shrugged. It was as though he was saying: *'Okay, fella. Have it your way. But I think you're a sucker for being so soft with a dame.'*

A few minutes later she came out from the bedroom, eyes downcast, cheeks still flushed. Without looking at either of us, she climbed into her coat, reached for her handbag. Still without looking at me, she asked: 'Shall we go now?'

'Yeah,' I gritted.

I opened the door for her with elaborate and mocking courtesy. She passed out quickly, head lowered, and it wasn't until she was halfway along the corridor I realised she hadn't said goodnight to Jackson.

That didn't break my heart.

She walked slowly and carefully down the stairs, turned to me when we reached the pavement and said, still without looking at me: 'I'm sorry about this, Hank.'

'I'll take you home,' I said bitterly. 'I'll call a taxi.'

There wasn't one in sight.

'We'll wait until one passes,' I said.

We started walking. She tried to take my arm. I pulled away from her, quickly, savagely. Her voice was pained. 'You hate me, don't you?' she said.

Sure I hated her. I hated her for the hot, unquenched desire inside me, the bitterness of frustration and the hurt of my pride. But I said proudly: 'No, sister, I don't hate you. I just don't want you touching me. I don't want you near me. You're kinda …

unclean!'

She said in a whisper: 'I don't blame you, Hank. That's the way I feel myself ... unclean!'

I heard the soft purr of a taxi, turned around and flagged it down into the kerbside. I opened the door for her, and she climbed inside. I gave the taxi driver her address and climbed in after her, shut the door.

She was sitting in the centre of the seat. When I sat down I was alongside her, touching her. I pushed myself to the far end of the seat, crushed myself up in the corner.

She said in a choked voice: 'You can't feel any worse about this than I do. Maybe it's too much to expect you to understand. Maybe it's too much for any guy to understand or forgive.'

'You don't owe me explanations,' I gritted. 'You're just a cheap dame, a cheap pick-up. There's plenty of your kind around. I don't have to break my heart on your account.'

Her voice was dead now. She said quietly but clearly: 'I know everything's changed between us, Hank. But it's finished now. Nothing can change it. I can only plead with you to help me as you promised to help me.'

Help you, hell! I thought. I said insultingly: 'I don't know any clients I can bring you!'

I heard her quick intake of breath. There was a silence while she allowed the sting of the insult to die away. Then she said clearly: 'John Maitland isn't dead.'

'That's right,' I said. 'Neither is Julius Caesar. They were both sitting on high stools at the counter in the Duberry tonight, drinking rye and dry ginger.'

She went on talking firmly and clearly, like I'd not interrupted. 'That wasn't John Maitland's body in the morgue. I knew immediately I saw it. And because

Jackson identified him, and he swore he was John Maitland, there was something fishy about him.'

'So you were suspicious of Jackson,' I jeered. 'That's the most original reason to date I've heard for a dame climbing between the sheets with a guy.'

'It was my only way to prove it,' she said tonelessly, like she was dead inside. 'Jackson was tall, he had the kinda arrogance and conceit that my sister wrote about. And what happened tonight was the only way I could prove it.'

'Prove what?' I sneered.

'Prove Jackson is really John Maitland.'

I wanted to laugh out loud. Then suddenly I didn't. Because it was slowly dawning on me Betty was undergoing a great strain. Her voice was tired and weary, like she'd exhausted herself, yet it kinda rang with conviction. I dropped being insulting and jeering. I asked: 'What makes you say a crazy thing like that?'

'Because he's got the birthmark on his right hip,' she said simply. 'Just the way Pat described it. That proves it. Me and Pat were as close as two sisters could be. She told me everything about Maitland, even to that funny little birthmark on his right hip.'

I'd pushed myself away from the corner and was leaning towards her with sudden interest. I rasped angrily: 'Who are you trying to kid? What d'you figure you'll get out of this?'

She turned to face me. I could dimly see her eyes gleaming through the darkness. Her head was high and her voice clear. 'I'm trying to tell you, Hank,' she said steadily. 'Jackson is really John Maitland. I proved it tonight. I've seen that birthmark *with my own eyes*. I've still got the letters Pat wrote, describing everything about him. And if you don't believe me, there's nothing I can do about it except to say, I'm sorry.'

It was crazy.

Her whole story was crazy.

How could John Maitland be Jackson? How could a black-bearded guy be a fair-headed crew-cut? Yet even as I doubted, my overworked brain was figuring how it could be worked. A fair-headed guy could grow a beard and grow his hair long. He could dye his beard and his hair. And later he could bleach himself again, shave off his beard and crop his hair to change his appearance.

I reached out through the darkness, hooked my fingers around her wrists, squeezed so hard I heard her wince. 'There's more in this than you're telling me,' I gritted. 'This guy Jackson or Maitland or whatever you choose to call him, he means something to you. You're bitter about the guy. If you wanna convince me, you can do so. Tell me why you're so set on finding him.'

There was a long pause before she said simply: 'I'll do that if you're willing to help. Help is what I need now. I need it badly. I'll tell you what you want to know if you'll promise to help.'

'Convince me,' I gritted. 'Then I'll help.'

'Come up to my apartment with me,' she said quietly. 'I'll prove it to you.'

This was probably just one more stall. An angle to get me into her apartment so she could sweeten me up. But if she did work that way, I'd pretty soon show her the way I felt. After what I'd seen. I didn't want to touch her. Not even while wearing rubber gloves.

'You convince me, then,' I said bitterly. 'If you can!'

I paid off the taxi, followed up the stairs to her apartment, followed her inside.

'Would you like a drink?' she asked tiredly.

'Just convince me,' I said heavily.

She went across to a small writing desk, opened it up, dug down at the back of the desk and brought back a large envelope. She drew out from it a photograph, passed it to me. 'Look at that,' she said.

I looked at it. It was a good photograph, glossy and well-printed. The subject was good too. The dame was vaguely familiar, beautifully proportioned, clean-limbed and healthy. She'd been photographed in an artistic pose. She was nude. The female body can be really beautiful when it is artistically photographed.

'So what?' I gritted.

'That's my sister,' she said, and the pain in her voice made me flash a quick glance at her.

'I can see the likeness,' I said, a little more gently.

'Now look at the others,' she said in a choked voice, and thrust the envelope at me, turned away like she couldn't bear to see me looking at them.

I drew out the first half a dozen of the photographs. I looked at them carefully and then thrust them back in the envelope quickly. I'd seen enough. The subject of the photographs was still Betty's sister. But she quite obviously hadn't posed, hadn't even known those photographs were being taken. A dame in the intimacy of her bedroom, shut away from the world while dressing and undressing, would die if she knew photographs were being taken of her every movement.

'These photographs were taken without Pat knowing,' I said.

Betty had her shoulders to me. Her voice was toneless. 'Maitland lived with her. He spied on her, took those photographs. She knew nothing about it.'

I shuffled my feet uncomfortably. 'That's kinda tough,' I said. 'Yet I don't see ...'

She spun around to face me, eyes blazing and

cheeks flaming. 'The negatives,' she snarled. 'Maitland's still got those negatives. There's always creepy, crawling, vile specimens who pay money for photographs like that. Selling photographs was how Maitland made his living, and I've got to stop him.' She grasped the lapels of my jacket, shook me hard and vigorously. 'You've gotta help,' she said fiercely, almost hysterically. 'I've gotta get those negatives from him. You see what he's doing. My sister's been driven to suicide, but he's still doing this dreadful thing, circulating her photographs to all those awful, leering, unhealthy men who ...'

I caught hold of her wrists, shook her hard. 'Cut it out,' I shouted. 'Shut up, will you? Get yourself under control.'

My voice shocked her back to reality. She pulled her wrists away from me, sank down into a chair. There was a hurt, choked note in her voice. 'I had to find him,' she said. 'I had to get those negatives. Maybe you understand now. I had to do it for Pat. And tonight ...' There was a sob in her throat. 'Tonight with Jackson was the only way to be sure he was Maitland.'

My brain was humming like a power station. I shook a cigarette from its packet, lit up slowly. 'You got that letter from your sister?'

'I'll get it,' she said quietly.

There was a big bundle of letters. She sorted through them, found one and handed it to me. I read it through slowly and carefully three times. It was just the way a young, excited dame would write. I read:

'*I know you'll think me simply dreadful, dear Betty, but I simply must tell you these things, even though I know how much you disapprove. He's such a dear, so tender and so thoughtful. And there's the cutest little ... I simply must tell you, because it tickled me so much ... the cutest little*

*birthmark on his right hip. And what do you think, darling?;
it's just exactly like a butterfly has been pasted on him. My
own darling, I just can't tell you how happy I am ...'*

I folded up the letter, put it back in the envelope. I
said: 'But this is crazy. Why should ...' I broke off
abruptly, stared into space.

Betty said dully: 'I don't know why he's done it. I
just know the facts. Jackson is Maitland. But whoever he
is, he's got possession of those negatives. And I must
have those negatives.'

My brain was ticking over at top speed. Suddenly
the wildest, craziest ideas were taking shape, forming
themselves. I was testing those ideas and they were
standing up to the test, forming shape so that a surge of
excitement was pulsing through me.

I reached for the envelope containing the
photographs. I took out the top one, the one showing
Betty's sister posed artistically. 'Can I keep this?'

Her brown eyes looked up hopefully. 'You think
you can do something, Hank?'

'Yeah,' I said. I stuffed the envelope into my
pocket. 'I'm beginning to see things,' I said. 'Merely a
matter of substitution.' I was thinking: *'Good old Billy.
Maybe you've tricked the* Chicago Chronicle *and everyone
else in Chicago. But you've given me an answer. You've
signposted a road.'*

She climbed to her feet. 'Hank,' she said softly. 'If
you can forgive me ... if you can do something for me.'
Her eyes dropped. 'I know how you must feel. I can only
say that I'll be terribly, terribly grateful.'

I took a coupla paces towards the door. 'You've got
my brain working,' I said detachedly. 'If I can sleep
tonight, I'll wake up in the morning with a clear head,
see everything crystal clear.'

She followed me to the door, stood so close she almost touched me when I opened it up. 'I'm sorry, Hank,' she whispered. 'I know it doesn't help, but I really am sorry.'

'Just stick around,' I said. 'Maybe I'll have news for you.' I was all worked up inside, fired by this new but crazy idea.

She swayed close, rested her hand gently on my arm. Instinctively I jerked my arm away like her touch burned. It musta hurt like I'd cut her across the cheek with a whip. She flinched, eyes pained and pathetic. 'Hank,' she said hoarsely. 'Hank!'

I stared into her tragic, brown eyes, understood something of the ordeal she'd undergone.

'I'm sorry, kid,' I said gently.

'Will it always be the same?' she whispered. 'Will you … always … remember?'

'It's kinda fresh, kid,' I said. 'I'm raw all over inside, flinching at the touch of a feather.'

'I didn't want to hurt you this way,' she whispered.

'Time's a great healer, kid,' I said gently. I reached out, touched her cheek gently with my finger. 'Maybe tomorrow will be a different day.'

'I hope so, Hank,' she said sincerely. 'I hope so.'

She stood at the door of her apartment, watched me as I walked along the corridor, watched me as I clattered down the stairway.

My brain was ticking over like a well-oiled, precision machine. I was checking and cross-checking, theorising and finding my theories held water. Yet the set-up was so well-planned, so ingenious it was staggering.

I was due to have a sleepless night anyway, on

account of my frustrated impulses. I decided to spend the night hours listening to my brain click over, testing again and again to find the weakness in my wild hunch.

And as I climbed into the taxi and gave the driver my address, I was thinking to myself:

'Good old Billy. Good old substitution!'

15

Half the night I'd lain awake in a kinda coma, midway between sleep and consciousness. Thought was all tangled up, Lucy and Betty edging their curves into my mind so it was difficult to concentrate. Everything milled around in my brain as I lay in the darkness; black-bearded guys with crew-cut fair hair, fragile, slipping shoulder-straps, and mysterious, enchanting cleavages; dead guys without faces who didn't have birthmarks, and Lucy's blue eyes inviting me to tug at slender strands of black silk.

Yet when I woke up in the morning, confusion had somehow marshalled itself into coherency. As soon as my eyes opened, my first thought was of photographs. Photographs and Joe Bates.

That's the mainspring.

But Joe Bates wasn't the starting point. It was a Sunday, which gave me the day off but meant I'd have to do the leg work by myself. It looked like being a lot of digging and it looked like being hard work.

I showered, made coffee, dressed myself in a grey suit and drove over to Superintendent Williams's cemetery. But it wasn't Superintendent Williams I wanted to see. On the contrary, I was hoping I wouldn't see him when I parked my car and followed the gravel path that led up to the church, went around the back door and dug out the records clerk so I could give him ten bucks.

The power of ten bucks is amazing. You don't have to be a millionaire to rule the world. All you need is a handful of ten dollar bills.

The ten bucks invited me inside his office, where I sat down with the cemetery records and spent three-quarters of an hour going through them.

It wasn't such a tough job as I'd expected. I chose a period, covering a week. During that week there'd been just over twenty burials. I took a note of all the burial names, and was grateful the names of the undertakers were also mentioned in the records. It made it even easier that just six different undertakers handled between them those twenty burials.

But just the same, six undertakers are a lot of guys to interview in one day. Especially when it is a Sunday.

I worked through the list steadily and conscientiously. The first undertaker had his shutters clamped down tightly. He'd gone off for the day with his family, and there were only a coloured maid and a dog in the house. The maid was scared to do anything out of line, but the sight of that crinkling ten dollar bill worked like a miracle drug. She nervously showed me into the office, stood there watching me while I went through the books, found the workshop sheets and checked them with my list.

The second undertaker was putting in overtime. He eyed me suspiciously. 'What's behind this?' he demanded.

'That's right,' I said grimly. 'Be smart, be awkward,

be as awkward as you can. Then see what happens.'

His eyes were still suspicious, but now he was uneasy too. 'What happens?' he asked cautiously.

'We do it just the same,' I told him. 'But we ask the questions down at headquarters instead of here. Sometimes it isn't comfortable at headquarters.'

He saw the red light. He didn't even ask to see my police credentials, which was a relief.

I checked with him the names of the folk he had buried. I checked the sizes of the coffins, the numbers of the grave and the cause of death.

'Anything else you need?' he asked resentfully.

'That's all, I guess.' I closed my little black notebook, snapped the elastic band around it and thrust it back in my breast pocket.

Two undertakers, and it had taken just over two hours. It took me another five hours to do the next four. By that time, I was good and tired and hungry. I found a café, ordered myself steak and eggs, mulled over the records I'd tabulated while I was waiting to be served.

I had to take into consideration every factor, the measurements of the coffins, the date of burial and the reason of death.

The state of the grave was something I had to return to the cemetery to check on.

I arrived back there with my list of suspects reduced by calculation to four. I wandered around the cemetery, tracing the grave numbers, found that three of my suspects were buried in family graves and one of them in a vault.

That made me feel a whole lot better. Because my wild hunch was being confirmed in every detail the deeper I dug. I was pretty certain now which was my suspect. But I'd gone as far as I could alone, and from this point I had to have professional assistance to prove me right.

I figured I knew a way to get help and at the same time apply just one more test to my wild hunch.

I drove to Joe Bates's apartment where he lived with Janet, knuckled the panels hard and waited impatiently for him to open up.

It was a Sunday evening and he'd been dozing in his chair, with the Sunday newspaper in his lap, a glass of beer at his elbow, and comfortable in slippers, collarless shirt and pants suspenders.

He stared at me apprehensively, a worried little man.

'Remember me?' I asked.

He nodded. He wasn't happy. 'Sure. I remember you.'

'Let's have a talk,' I suggested gently.

'I guess so,' he replied dismally.

I followed him inside, made myself comfortable opposite. 'Are we alone?'

'Janet's gone out with Red,' he said unhappily.

I leaned forward, said earnestly: 'You had a raw deal with the cops, didn't you? They hung a rap on you. When did you get out? Yesterday?'

'Yeah,' he said gloomily. 'Yesterday.'

'But you weren't guilty, were you?' I persisted.

His soulful eyes stared into mine dejectedly. 'How am I ever gonna prove that?'

'You wanna prove it?'

For the first time, I saw a hint of indignation and anger breaking through his resignation. 'What d'you think?' he snarled. 'Janet thinks I'm one of those guys who carries around ...'

'She doesn't,' I said quietly. 'She has the utmost

faith in you.'

'I'd just like to prove to her I'm not that kind of guy.'

'You can,' I said gently. 'If you want, you can prove it.'

His eyes lighted up, and then died to dull resignation. 'How?' he said hopelessly. 'How can I prove it?'

'You've heard of me, Joe,' I said persuasively. 'I'm Hank Janson.' I thrust my reporter's card under his nose. 'You've gotta understand the way it is, Joe. You've gotta take my word for everything. But you can trust me. Most guys who aren't on the straight know they can trust me when I give my word.'

There was a gleam of interest in his dull eyes now. 'What d'ya wanna know?'

'The cemetery where you were picked up,' I said. 'It was Meadowside cemetery, wasn't it?'

He nodded dismally.

I nodded with satisfaction. It was Superintendent Williams's cemetery.

'What were you doing there that night, Joe?'

His eyes were dull. 'Just like I told them. I climbed over into the cemetery for a joke. I found the photographs, put them in my pocket.'

I leaned forward, tapped him on the knee with my forefinger. 'I'm not kidding you, Joe. String along with me and I can probably prove you weren't guilty of that rap.'

Again that gleam of interest in his eyes. 'You wouldn't kid a guy?'

'I'm on the level, Joe. Anything you tell me doesn't go further than me unless you want.'

He took a deep breath. 'Okay,' he said. 'I'll tell you

the way it was. I was gonna get a hundred bucks for this, see. A guy I knew pulled the job the night before. A safe job. All dough except for a little chamois leather bag containing a handful of uncut diamonds. This guy I knew got worried, buried the chamois bag in Meadowside, because he figured first thing in the morning the cops would be around to his joint, asking questions.'

'The notes he hid away somewhere else?' I guessed.

'That's right. Didn't want his eggs all in one basket.'

'And you had to grab the diamonds from the cemetery and hold them for him?'

He nodded. 'He got in touch with me the next morning, telephoned from a kiosk. Said he'd give me a hundred bucks to keep them safe for him a coupla weeks.'

'Okay, Joe,' I said. 'Now come clean. Tell me exactly what happened.'

'On the phone I musta got the wrong grave number,' he said dolefully. 'When I got there, it wasn't the way he described it at all. He'd said it was a cross on a stone block, and he'd dug a small hole at the right hand top corner. But the grave I found was just a plain headstone.' His sad face sagged visibly. 'Just my luck.'

'The photographs,' I encouraged gently.

'I gave up,' he said. 'I was on the way back when I saw this vault with the door open. You know how careful they are about these things. Vault doors are always locked. So I investigated.'

'What was there, Joe?' I said tensely. 'What did you find?'

'Nothing,' he said glumly. 'Just a vault with maybe

half a dozen coffins on the shelves inside. And that envelope was on the floor. I felt it with my foot, saw it was an envelope, picked it up quickly and put it in my pocket, and then got out of there quickly.' His sad eyes pleaded for sympathy. 'It kinda gave me the creeps inside that vault. Those stiffs lying quietly in their boxes on the shelves. It kinda hit me suddenly. I didn't know a guy could get scared like that. Maybe it was on account of some of those Dracula films I've seen. I suddenly imagined those fellas inside the coffins tapping away at the lids, trying to get out, trying to wind their long bony arms around me.' Again he sighed. 'I got out of there real quick. Maybe if I hadn't have been so scared, I'd have looked first, instead of escaping right into the arms of those cops.'

'You've seen those photographs, haven't you, Joe?' I asked gently.

He looked at me almost indignantly. 'What do you think? I went to jail on account of them.'

I pulled the photograph of Betty's sister from my pocket, showed it to him. 'What d'you make of that?'

He stared at it. Then he stared at me. 'That's the same dame. Only this is different. If they'd all been like this, it wouldn't have mattered.'

I leaned forward, spoke to him intently and sincerely. 'You help me and I'll help you,' I promised him. 'Tonight I can get proof you know nothing about those photographs. I'll prove it right up to the hilt. But you've gotta help me.'

Interest was burning in his eyes. 'Listen, fella,' he said. 'I feel real bad about all this. Janet's a sweet kid. She knows I've been a crook, she knows I've stolen and been to jail. But this is different. This kinda offence is a rotten, despicable thing for a guy to have hanging over him. Especially when his wife's sister ...'

'You can help me, Joe,' I said. 'You know how to do it. That's why I need you.'

'How to do what?'

'Open the locked door of a vault.'

He stared at me.

I stared at him.

'What are you driving at?' he asked in a hoarse whisper.

I told him.

I hadn't been wrong about Joe Bates. He was a little guy, but like most little guys he had guts. He said he would string along with me, and from then onwards we just sat and talked, waiting for the time to pass.

About eight o'clock that evening, Janet returned home with Red. Janet was coldly polite, her attitude reminding me that I'd been a heel not doing anything about getting Joe Bates out of jail.

Red was frankly aggressive. He grunted at me, sat in a corner while Janet busied herself preparing a meal, watched me with angry, contemptuous eyes. They both showed plainly they wondered what I wanted with Joe Bates. Janet was too proud to ask, and me and Joe kept our mouths clamped tight, pulled our chairs up to the table, the four of us eating without exchanging a word.

We thawed out a little after dinner. Janet suggested a game of gin rummy, and we played until half past twelve in the morning. Then I caught Joe's eye, and casually he climbed to his feet, said in a flat voice: 'I'll walk along with you, Hank.'

Janet and Red exchanged swift, suspicious glances. Neither of them said anything.

Joe went through to the bedroom, came out a little later, shrugging into his slicker.

'Don't wait up for me, Janet,' said Joe. 'Hank and me are gonna meet some old friends.'

Janet's eyes stared at Joe steadily, then switched to me. She said, with a hurt note in her voice: 'You're not going to get into trouble, are you, Joe?'

He laughed scoffingly, patted her on the shoulder affectionately. 'Don't be silly, kid,' he chided. 'I shan't be long. It's just that I don't want you to over-tire yourself. You've work tomorrow.'

'I'm going soon anyway,' grunted Red. His eyes never left me for a moment. That red-headed kid made me feel more guilty and ashamed than I'd felt for a long time.

'How do we get there?' asked Joe when we got outside.

'Walk,' I said. 'It's early yet and it'd be crazy parking my car outside.' Another thought came to me. 'Have you got everything you need?'

He tapped the pockets of his slicker. 'Got it right here.'

'Good,' I grunted.

We took our time, stopped on the way to drink coffee at a night café, finally brought up outside the walls of the cemetery at half past one.

The street lighting was bad in that neck of the woods. We waited for maybe five minutes, listening for footsteps, and then I said crisply: 'Okay. You go first, Joe.'

I gave him a leg-up. He was like a monkey, swinging himself up and over with amazing agility. I sprang up, felt my fingers curl over the lip of the wall, hung for a moment with the weight of my body tearing my arms from my sockets. I flexed my muscles, drew myself up until my chin was level with the top of the wall, drew myself even higher until I could swing my leg up and over, straddling the wall like a horse.

Joe was waiting for me in the darkness the other side, grasped my arm with uncanny certainty as my shoes hit the soft earth.

'This way,' he urged.

'I know,' I told him. 'I know.'

It was the first time I'd been in a cemetery at night. But the quietness, the darkness and the white headstones all around me made me feel something of the cold, clammy apprehension that musta sent Joe scampering fear-stricken from the vault.

I ain't a jumpy guy, but that sure was a place to give a guy the creeps.

I didn't feel any better when we reached the door of the vault and Joe produced a coupla tools, started opening it, metal clinking against metal.

It was maybe ten minutes before something gave. Then the door kinda creaked, and it swung open on squealing hinges.

'Okay,' I said. 'In you go.'

'You go first,' said Joe with suspicious politeness.

I took a deep breath, plunged down the steps into the dark interior of the vault. Joe crowded close behind me like he felt better treading on my heels.

I fumbled in my pocket, drew out a small flash torch and flicked it around the vault.

There were seven coffins there, cold, silent and somehow resentful of our intrusion.

Six of them were thick with dust. The seventh, the most recent, was new and shiny, the handles untarnished.

'That's the one, Joe,' I whispered.

In the dim light of the flashlamp I could see he was sweating. He moved over to the coffin, stood looking down at it for a long while, took a grip on himself, fitted a screwdriver into the brass-headed screws with trembling hands and began turning.

The screws came out easily; surprisingly easy. Even that supported my theory.

When there was just one more screw to be removed, Joe wiped his hand across his forehead, handed me the screwdriver. 'You take over now,' he said.

If Joe's sweating was like mine, it wasn't on account he was hot. I wore a film of cold sweat that chilled me, made me feel bad inside, made my fingers shake as I took the screwdriver from him.

That last screw was the longest screw in the world, seemed to turn and turn, growing ever upwards from the coffin lid like it was never gonna stop coming out. I was half-hoping it wouldn't.

'Okay, that's it, Joe,' I said at last.

'I sure hope your hunch is right,' he breathed.

'It's gotta be,' I gritted. 'It's gotta be.'

He moved to the head of the coffin, grasped the lid. I took the other end. 'Ready,' I said. My voice was a hoarse croak.

'Ready,' he croaked back.

We lifted off the lid, set it down alongside the coffin. I shone the torch inside, got a momentary pang of alarm when I saw the face wasn't showing.

I was certain now I was right. Yet it needed tremendous will-power to take that white swathing in my hands and tear it apart. Then I breathed a sigh of relief.

Joe Bates stared, gulped. 'It's earth,' he said. 'It's full of earth.'

'Which proves I'm right,' I panted.

A voice spoke in the same moment. A powerful flashlight beam bathed both of us. 'But which also proves you weren't cautious enough,' said the voice.

I turned swiftly, blinking in the strong white glare. That light was powerful, prevented me from seeing who bulked behind the torch.

Not that it mattered. I'd have recognised the voice anywhere. 'It was smart figuring, Janson,' said Jackson.

'Yeah,' I panted. I shot a swift glance at Joe Bates, wondering if he'd go in with me if I tackled Jackson.

But it was Jackson who interpreted my glance.

'I wouldn't do it, Janson,' he advised gently. 'This automatic holds six shots. That's three slugs apiece. And right now, I'd take a chance on the shots being heard.'

'You're washed up, Jackson,' I told him. 'I've got it all figured. You're sewn up tight now.'

From behind the flashlight beam I heard another voice; a plaintive, frightened voice. 'He's on to us,' panted Superintendent Williams. There was an hysterical note in his voice. 'He's figured it out some way. We've gotta get away. We've gotta beat it. I told you this was too risky.'

'Shuddup,' snarled Jackson.

'We've gotta get away,' panted Williams. 'It's hopeless. They all know now.'

'Quit whining and leave this to me,' snarled Jackson. His voice rasped at me and Bates along the powerful beam. 'You're coming up out of that vault. I want you to come straight out and walk straight ahead. I'll tell you when to stop walking.'

He backed away from us up the steps, keeping the

light trained on us. 'All right,' he snarled. 'Come on up.'

I looked at Joe expressively. He stared back at me, shrugged his shoulders. Grimly, I walked towards the flashlight, slowly climbed the steps. The flashlight moved ahead of me, went over to the left. Jackson growled: 'Just keep walking straight ahead. And remember. I'm not scared of taking a chance on using this gun.'

There was nothing for it. I kept walking straight ahead like he told me. Joe Bates followed, and Jackson and Williams circled around back of us, followed behind us, searchlighting us all the time in that powerful light.

Jackson herded us straight across the cemetery, following the lanes between the gravestones, growling at us until we brought up before another brick-built vault. I could tell by the worn marble and the green moss on the outside that it musta been at least a hundred years old.

I didn't like the look of that vault. Neither did Bates. We both hesitated. 'G'wan,' growled Jackson. 'Get down them steps.'

Reluctantly, unwillingly, I stumbled down the steps, Bates right behind me. The door was a solid, rusted iron. 'Push it,' gritted Jackson. 'It's open.'

I thrust at it, and the hinges squealed as it yawned open on to enveloping blackness.

'Right, inside,' instructed Jackson.

I took a coupla paces into the darkness, then flinched back as I sensed movement, heard a muttered gasp from the blackness ahead of me. Then the flashlight was angling down, revealing the inside of the vault.

I felt a lump rise in my throat.

She stared at me with wide, terrified eyes. Her hair was dishevelled, blood and dust streaked her cheek and forehead, and she was huddled on the floor at the far end of the vault. The way she had her hands behind her showed she was pinioned to an iron shackle cemented low down in the wall.

'Right inside,' snarled Jackson.

I pushed further inside, Joe Bates crowding behind me.

'Right to the far end,' instructed Jackson. 'Then both of you sit on the floor with your backs against the wall.'

When a desperate guy's got a revolver pointing at your spine, you don't argue.

I settled on the floor alongside Betty, felt the cold of the floor strike up through my pants, heard Betty choke: *'Thank heavens you're here, Hank.'*

Joe settled down beside me. Being spotlighted by that torch and sitting on the floor made us helpless, defenceless targets.

Jackson said from the doorway: 'You figured it fine, Janson. But you weren't smart enough.'

I tipped my fedora to the back of my head with my forefinger, said wearily: 'You won't get far, Jackson. Maybe you'll win yourself a few hours' respite, enough to get a mile or two ahead of the cops. But they'll get you in the end. You won't get away with this.'

My eyes were becoming accustomed to the bright glare now. I could see the dim outline of Jackson behind the torch. Behind him, hovering uncertainly, was the shadowy outline of Williams.

'You're smart about most things, Janson,' he rasped. 'But you're not being over-smart about this. You're missing the obvious.'

'Meaning what?'

'Figure where you are,' he said. 'This is an old vault, hasn't been used for thirty years. No claims are being made on it any more. It's due to be walled in.'

Suddenly that vault became much darker, much damper, much colder, too. I was beginning to realise how crazy I was to have walked in there so meekly instead of making a desperate dive for Jackson and taking a chance on getting that gun from him.

'Don't worry,' he said sadistically. 'You won't know anything about the walling-in.. None of you will know about it. With this door closed and a coupla blocks of sulphur smouldering in the air vent, you won't wanna know anything except how quick you can choke your lungs up and die peacefully.'

I'd seen sulphur used once. Just a small piece the size of a lump of sugar, set alight and left in a sealed kitchen. A coupla hours later there wasn't a cockroach or any other insect alive in that kitchen. And it took forty-eight hours for the opened windows and doors to ventilate the room clean again.

Jackson wouldn't use small cubes of sulphur. He'd use maybe a pound or more, stacked right in the air vent while the three of us were inside, coughing, choking and suffocating to death like trapped vermin.

I flexed my muscles, pressed my heels into the cold stone floor, tensed to launch myself at Jackson in a crazy, desperate, suicide tackle.

And even as I tensed, I saw the third shadow looming up behind Jackson, poising and launching itself through the air.

The flashlight jerked, jumped towards me, described an arc through the air, hit the stone floor and rolled without going out. In the same moment, I was in movement, hurtling into the darkness, my shoulders crashing into Jackson's thighs. As I grappled with him, brought him thudding to the ground, a voice I knew was grating: 'Get him, Janson. I've got his arms. Sock him, will ya?'

It was Red. That young, ginger-haired kid had loomed up out of the night, united his natural aggressiveness with mine, tipping the scales of death balanced against me.

I clawed out into the darkness, touched a head that was cropped short. I spread my fingers around the head, held it firmly in position, brought over my left with all the strength I had, gauging accurately, feeling my knuckles pound bone, hearing his teeth snap together.

I did it again. And then a third time. The fourth time wasn't necessary, but I did it just the same.

I climbed to my feet, dived for the flashlight. I swung it around, and there was Jackson lying on the stone floor, eyes closed and blood trickling from his mashed lips. Red stood over him, fists poised, ready to take him if he showed signs of movement. Just within range of the flashlight was Williams. A pale-faced, sweating Williams, whose eyes were starting from his head as little Joe Bates crooked his arm around his neck from behind, held a pointed screwdriver against his throat. The touch of that cold steel had got Williams's knees buckling beneath him in fear.

I picked up Jackson's gun, levelled it at Williams, motioned to Bates to release him.

'Okay, Williams,' I gritted. 'Over there in the corner.'

He scuttled into the corner like a scared rabbit, sat on the floor with his back against the wall.

'Release the dame,' I told Joe.

Betty's wrists were chafed and painful, and she was shaky on her legs, had to lean against the wall when she stood up.

'Nice work, Red,' I rasped. 'This guy Jackson's the one we're likely to have trouble with. Help me drag him over there, tie him up, the way he tied the dame.'

Not until Jackson was firmly secured did I breathe easily. I wasn't worried about Williams. I merely had to point my gun and he nearly fainted.

'How d'you feel, kid?' I asked Betty.

She passed one hand across her forehead. 'A little better now.'

'Listen, Joe,' I said. 'I'm not taking risks. You go call the cops. Bring them right back here.'

'Sure you can manage alone?' he asked.

I grinned. He was a little guy. But he had guts. I didn't resent him being doubtful of my ability to handle these two guys.

'Sure, Joe,' I said. 'I'll be okay. You go get the cops.'

Jackson moaned, his eyes blinked and then closed again.

Joe gave him a regretful look, like he'd like to have socked Jackson himself, before he scuttled up the steps and out of the vault.

'How come you happen to be around?' I asked Red.

'I figured there was something screwy,' he panted. 'You and Joe going off together. I kinda trailed along. Looks like it was lucky I did.'

'It sure was lucky,' I said sincerely.

Betty came across to me, leaned against me. I put my arm around her, felt her yielding softness, and liked it.

Red said aggressively: 'Listen, Janson. I horned in when it looked like it was necessary. But what the hell's it all about, anyway?'

'It's a little involved,' I told him.

'Try me,' he said sarcastically. 'Tell me it nice and easy in single syllable words. Maybe I'll understand.'

I nodded towards Williams. 'That guy was due to collect two hundred grand if his wife died. But it wasn't a secret. Everybody knew how much he had to gain if his wife kicked the bucket. So anytime his wife came to an unnatural end, Williams was the first suspect.'

'She committed suicide, didn't she?'

'That's what Williams wanted everyone to think.' I nodded towards Jackson. 'But this guy figured out a move that was really smart. So smart he had everyone fooled.

'He figured if Williams's wife ran off with some guy and they both committed suicide, it would give Williams a first class let-out.'

'So he just hunted around for a guy who was willing to commit suicide,' sneered Red.

I eyed him solemnly. 'You're not thinking deeply enough, Red. It had to be more subtle than that. And it wasn't something that could be done in a hurry. Jackson spent eighteen months building up the background for it. He went away, grew his hair long and grew a beard. He dyed his hair and his beard black, gave himself the name of John Maitland and began creating the living character of John Maitland.' I breathed hard. 'Jackson really worked at it, too. He got himself involved with three dames, made an income on the side from selling photographs.' I sensed Red tauten. 'Photographs of dames he was promising to marry. The same photographs that Joe picked up that night here in the cemetery.'

Red's voice was baffled. 'I don't get it. How can Jackson be John Maitland and commit suicide and still be here?'

'Substitution,' I said gently. 'Substitution. Williams's wife had to die. To make it good she had to die with somebody – a suicide pact. That somebody was John Maitland. But it wasn't really John Maitland, and it wasn't Jackson either. It was somebody planted with John Maitland's identification papers in his pocket and John Maitland's background grafted on to him.'

He stared at me.

'Don't you get it yet?' I said. 'Williams is superintendent of this cemetery. All he had to do was await the opportune moment. He needed a dark-haired guy, six feet tall. He kept tabs on all the guys buried, and when a dark-haired, six foot fella became a candidate for this vault, that dropped everything into Williams's and Jackson's lap.'

Betty was smarter than Red. She could see it all now. I sensed her shudder.

Red said doubtfully: 'You mean they took a dead guy, and ...'

'Exactly,' I interrupted. 'The day this vault was opened for its new inmate, Jackson and Williams were taking the body from its casket the same night. And for certain the same night Mrs Williams was killed.' I looked grimly at Williams, who was white-faced, eyes rolling, like he was crazy. 'The betting is Williams didn't have the nerve to kill her himself. Jackson must have done it for him.'

Red said with a note of disbelief in his voice: 'You mean they took them both, Williams's wife and the stiff, took them out to the country, hung bombs around their necks, and set them off?'

'The Mills bombs were necessary,' I said. 'They could substitute a body, but they couldn't substitute a face. But a faceless corpse with John Maitland's papers in his pocket and John Maitland's background could fool everyone. The only risk was the bodies being discovered too soon. Time had to elapse so the pathologist couldn't report with any certainty the time of death. Because Mrs Williams musta died a few days after the fella.'

Red said with a note of bafflement in his voice: 'It's kinda complicated, isn't it? It's kinda tricky to follow straight off. Would you do it again for me?'

I tightened my arm around Betty's waist. 'Not now, kid,' I said wearily. 'Read about it in the papers tomorrow.'

'You know what,' he said. 'It's kinda difficult to follow it even when you tell me.'

From the darkness we heard the distant sirens of the approaching cop car.

'Yeah,' I agreed. 'It is kinda complicated.'

He was thinking hard. 'If it's so tough to understand even when you know how it's done, how come you managed to figure it out yourself?'

I took a deep breath. 'I've been taking lessons. I've been given inside dope. I've been taught how to be clairvoyant.'

16

I guess Jackson's plot really was ingenious and complicated. Down at police headquarters, I had to go through it three times before they saw it clearly.

That meant it was four o'clock in the morning before they finished taking down evidence.

Then it took me three-quarters of an hour to map out a story for the *Chronicle* and phone it in to the rewrite man.

When I was through, Betty was still waiting for me.

'How d'ya feel, kid?' I asked.

'Take me home, will you, Hank?' she asked.

I took her home, escorted her right to the door of her apartment. Neither of us were tired. So much had happened, it made our brains over-active, too unsettled for sleep.

'How about a coffee?' she asked.

'Couldn't think of anything better.'

I sat and smoked while she busied herself, brought two big cups of strong, steaming coffee to the table.

I dropped three knobs of sugar into my cup,

stirred it thoughtfully. 'It hurts asking this,' I said, 'but I've got to ask it. Maybe it will hurt telling me. But I've gotta know.'

Her brown eyes eyed me steadily. 'What are you trying to say, Hank?'

'You went to Jackson's flat today. I know what you told the police, how you talked for a while and how he went out and came back unexpectedly, found you searching for the negatives. But I wanna know the truth. Did the same thing happen as yesterday …?'

Her brown yes didn't falter. 'No, Hank,' she said sincerely. 'I'd found out what I wanted to know. I flirted with him, strung him along, hoping for some chance to search for the negatives.'

I heaved a deep breath, exhaled slowly. 'You took a chance, kid. You shoulda left me to get those negatives for you.'

She said with a break in her voice: 'I thought that after yesterday you …'

'You did a crazy thing,' I said. 'The last thing you shoulda told Jackson when he found you searching was that you were looking for those negatives. That exposed everything. That proved to him you were the one person who knew he was John Maitland.'

'I didn't know as much then as you,' she pointed out. 'All that concerned me was those negatives.' She looked at me anxiously. 'Did the police find them when they searched?'

'You heard what Detective-Inspector Blunt promised,' I told her. 'Those cops will take Jackson's apartment to pieces. They'll find those negatives and they'll destroy them. If you want, you can go along and watch them destroyed. Blunt's a straight guy.

When he says a thing, he means it. You can rely on him.'

'And Jackson?' she asked. 'What will happen to him?'

'What usually happens to murderers?' I asked bluntly. 'They're both in it together. Williams and Jackson. They haven't got a wriggle.'

'He deserves it,' she said quietly. 'He deserves to die. He killed my sister as surely as though he had killed her with his own two hands.'

I finished my coffee, put the cup back in the saucer and climbed to my feet slowly. 'I'll be getting along,' I said.

She didn't try to stop me. She came to the door, touched my arm when I had my hand on the doorknob. This time I didn't jerk my arm away. Her brown eyes stared up into mine, searchingly. She said sincerely: 'I am going to see you again, aren't I, Hank?'

I looked down into her eyes. The events and strain of the last few hours seemed to have drained the strength from that physical demon inside me. 'Is that what you want?' I asked quietly.

'I want it if you want it.'

'You're gonna be around?'

'I'll be around, for a while ... if that's what you want.'

'I'll ring you,' I said.

Her brown eyes were misty. 'You still feel bad, Hank?' Her voice was a whisper.

'Yeah,' I admitted, and it was difficult to say the words, because my throat was constricted.

'I had to do it,' she whispered. 'You've got to understand that. It was torment for me knowing that Pat ...' She broke off.

'Sure, kid, I understand,' I said gently.

I don't know how it happened. Suddenly she was in my arms, pressing against me, arms encircling and fingers digging into my shoulders. 'I didn't want to be this way, Hank,' she half sobbed. 'I didn't want to make you feel bad. I didn't want to make myself feel unclean. Aren't you ever gonna get over it? Aren't you ever gonna forget it?'

I put my forefinger under her chin and tilted her face up towards mine. Her brown eyes were swimming with tears. 'I've gotta be the way I am,' I told her. 'I'm human. But it's time that counts. Yesterday I didn't want you to touch me. Today it's not so bad. Today I don't mind holding you close. But I need more time. Don't you understand that? Maybe tomorrow ...'

'I'll give you time, Hank,' she whispered.

'You're a smart kid,' I said. 'Because I can't force myself. I've just got to learn to accept what's happened.'

'I'll give you time, Hank,' she said again, tenderly. 'I'll be waiting.'

She stood at the door of her apartment, looking after me wistfully. She watched me all the way along the corridor, watched me walk down the stairs, smiling sadly and wistfully at me before the stairwell cut her off from my vision.

Outside in the cool night air, I drew a deep breath, exhaled it slowly through my teeth, then started walking briskly towards home.

A guy can't help the way he feels. But Betty was a nice kid. Maybe I could forget.

Maybe.

The thought was reassuring, because the

physical demon inside me had given me hell these last few days. It was good to know that when that demon flexed his muscles again, stirred himself strongly and compellingly, that there would be a way of meeting his pressing demands.

Yeah, I was thinking, as I strode through the night, my heels echoing along the silent sidewalks. *Betty is a cute kid. Maybe it won't take all that time to forget, at that.*

ALSO AVAILABLE FROM TELOS PUBLISHING

CRIME

THE LONG, BIG KISS GOODBYE
by SCOTT MONTGOMERY
Hardboiled thrills as Jack Sharp gets involved with a
dame called Kitty.

MIKE RIPLEY

Titles in Mike Ripley's acclaimed 'Angel' series of comic
crime novels.

JUST ANOTHER ANGEL by MIKE RIPLEY
ANGEL TOUCH by MIKE RIPLEY
ANGEL HUNT by MIKE RIPLEY
ANGEL ON THE INSIDE by MIKE RIPLEY
ANGEL CONFIDENTIAL by MIKE RIPLEY
ANGEL CITY by MIKE RIPLEY
ANGELS IN ARMS by MIKE RIPLEY
FAMILY OF ANGELS by MIKE RIPLEY
BOOTLEGGED ANGEL by MIKE RIPLEY
THAT ANGEL LOOK by MIKE RIPLEY

HANK JANSON

Classic pulp crime thrillers from the 1940s and 1950s.

TORMENT by HANK JANSON
WOMEN HATE TILL DEATH by HANK JANSON

SOME LOOK BETTER DEAD by HANK JANSON
SKIRTS BRING ME SORROW by HANK JANSON
WHEN DAMES GET TOUGH by HANK JANSON
ACCUSED by HANK JANSON
KILLER by HANK JANSON
FRAILS CAN BE SO TOUGH by HANK JANSON
BROADS DON'T SCARE EASY by HANK JANSON
KILL HER IF YOU CAN by HANK JANSON
LILIES FOR MY LOVELY by HANK JANSON
BLONDE ON THE SPOT by HANK JANSON
THIS WOMAN IS DEATH by HANK JANSON
THE LADY HAS A SCAR by HANK JANSON

Non-fiction

THE TRIALS OF HANK JANSON
by STEVE HOLLAND

TELOS PUBLISHING
Email: orders@telos.co.uk
Web: www.telos.co.uk

To order copies of any Telos books, please visit our
website where there are full details of all titles and
facilities for worldwide credit card online ordering, as
well as occasional special offers.